Died

And

Prejudice

A Cross-Town Books Mystery

By Elinor Battersby

Chapter 1

It is a truth universally acknowledged, that a single man in possession of an artisanal gin distillery, must be in want of a wife. Within the small community of Cross Street Cambridge, Mr Bingley certainly didn't lack for choice.

"You should get in there quickly Shelley, if you want to stand a chance! I already popped over and introduced myself days ago," Maggie announced cheerfully.

"I'm not *trying* to be *in with a chance*! Besides, I can't just go over there and introduce myself, that would be... embarrassing," Shelley replied, flushing up to the roots of her auburn hair.

"Darling, at my age you won't be so sensitive. Besides, it's good manners to welcome a new neighbour."

Maggie adjusted her silver grey curls as she spoke, watching as Shelley stacked books onto the shelves before them.

Heidi observed them both from her vantage point, behind the counter against the far wall of the shop. For all her talk of 'good manners' Heidi couldn't help noticing that Maggie was wearing even more sequins than usual and her hair looked freshly styled and set. She allowed herself a small smile before stepping back hastily out of sight when the older woman swung around to survey the room.

"Where's Heidi? She should get a wriggle on too! You can bet the rest of the ladies in the street wont have wasted any time!"

Shelley's reply was muttered at a low enough pitch that Heidi couldn't make it out, but she could easily imagine what the young woman might say. Heidi hadn't been on a date or shown any romantic inclination in all the time that Shelley had known her. She was unlikely to start now. Actually, Heidi hadn't shown any romantic inclinations in her life, beyond enjoying the perusal of the odd romance novel that is.

"Heidi?" Maggie called out.

Heidi remained fixed in place, hidden behind a wall of historical fiction. She knew that Maggie meant well, but even her gentle nudges and hints set Heidi on edge, and she didn't exactly seem to be in a gentle, nudging mood. After another moment Maggie clearly gave up, grumbled briefly, and then distracted herself by describing the delectable Mr Bingley for the dozenth time. It wasn't until the bell above the door sounded that Heidi was forced from her refuge.

"Hello ladies!" the new arrival crooned in a shrill

voice.

"Lydia. To what do we owe the pleasure?" Maggie asked in a slightly flattened voice.

"Just popping round to extend an invitation," Lydia told them magnanimously.

"An invitation?" Maggie repeated, clearly interested despite herself.

"I'm throwing a party dears, over at my shop on Friday. It seems like the right thing to do, to welcome our new neighbour and ensure that he feels like part of our little community here," she explained grandly, her scarlet nails running through her violently bleached hair so that it swung and settled around her shoulders.

"Getting your claws in, are you darling?" Maggie asked, her eyes twinkling.

"Sorry?"

"A party? What sort of party?!" Shelley cut in quickly.

"Black tie. Best glad-rags only. Is that going to be a problem Shells?" her voice dipped in deepest sympathy as she spoke and Shelley flushed crimson once again.

"No, that's fine," she murmured hurriedly.

"Of course it's fine, why wouldn't it be?!" Maggie demanded in steely accents.

Lydia pressed a hand to her own chest and gasped theatrically.

"A single parent whose husband *left* her?! I know that

money must be tight and the last thing in the world that I would want is to be insensitive!"

"Heaven forbid," Maggie commented drily.

"Anyway," Lydia continued happily, "I'm inviting everyone in the street. Spouses but no children, sorry Shells."

"It's Shelley dear. Not Shells. We can sound it out if you need, we are a book shop after all," Maggie offered sweetly.

"You certainly are, aren't you," Lydia agreed, casting a look of distaste at her surroundings.

Heidi silently bridled, stung against her will by Lydia's obvious disdain. Something of her thoughts must have shown in her manner because suddenly Lydia's attention fixed on her.

"Heidi! You're awfully quiet! You're invited to the party too of course, as a business owner..." she trailed off, her expression souring as it always did when she remembered that Heidi owned Cross-Town Books.

"Oh, I don't think so. Thank you though," she replied evenly, her words carefully chosen and measured so as not to cause offence.

"Nonsense! Of course you'll come!" Maggie countered hotly.

"She doesn't have to if she doesn't want to," Lydia retorted sharply.

"Afraid she'll cast you into the shade?" Maggie challenged, raising an eyebrow.

At these words, it was both Heidi and Lydia's turn to blush.

"I don't really enjoy parties," Heidi told them a little lamely.

"And how would you know that dear?" Maggie asked her straight. Blunt but not unkind.

"Parties aren't for everybody," Lydia sing-songed brightly, lifting herself up and tossing her hair in a way that clearly indicated that parties were most certainly for *her*.

"I should be able to come along on Friday," Shelley mused aloud, "You're hosting it at your shop?"

"I absolutely am! It's perfect! The space was designed to be used for events and my wares will lend the evening a certain something extra, don't you think?" Lydia giggled excitedly.

"A party surrounded with knickers and brassieres sounds indecent to me, but I suppose beggars can't be choosers. You'll have music? And food and drinks?" Maggie demanded.

"Yes of course," Lydia snapped, clearly not thrilled with this less than effusive reception of her plans.

"And Bingley is definitely going to be there?"

"He is. And the mysterious business partner too!" Lydia crowed triumphantly.

"Business partner?!"

"A Mr Darby apparently. I have it on good authority that he's the money behind the business," Lydia told them, breathing the word money as though it were the name of a lover.

"Ha! No wonder you're clamouring to put an event together!" Maggie barked, her small frame shaken by laughter.

"I just think it's important that this Mr Darby sees everything that Cross Street has to offer," she purred, rolling her shoulders slightly in a way that made Heidi feel vaguely uncomfortable.

"Oh I don't doubt you'll display everything you have to offer," Maggie chuckled.

Lydia's face froze and her shoulders hardened.

"I know it must be difficult being the little old lady in the street, Maggie, but no one likes a bitter old woman," she spat venomously.

"Lydia!" Shelley exclaimed scandalised.

"It's quite alright Shelley dear, when you reach the ripe old age of myself or our Lydia here, you wont let words ruffle you. Isn't that right Lydia?" Maggie asked the woman sweetly.

Lydia appeared to be lost for words. Her mouth hung open and her heavily kohled eyes protruded from her head.

"It's lovely of you to arrange a party for the young

people, I expect they'll have a wonderful time. Shelley and Heidi will certainly be attending. I'll pop round too of course, us old gals need to put in an appearance on the social scene, don't we," she continued on, happily surveying the effect that her words were having.

Lydia appeared to be taking on a purple hue, the colour sweeping up her neck and suffusing her face.

"LYDIA! YOU COW!"

A screech sounded, completely undisguised by the clamour of the bell over the door. Heidi took a half step back, the drama already reaching a near overwhelming pitch.

Shelley too looked wary, but Maggie's manner was all undisguised delight.

Lydia took a small breath and waited a beat before turning to greet the new arrival. When she did, she had plastered a smile back on her face and the beetroot tones were rapidly receding.

"Kitty, how are you?" she asked pleasantly.

"I TOLD YOU I WANTED TO THROW A PARTY!" Kitty screeched, still at full volume.

"Did you?" Lydia queried disinterestedly, examining the scarlet polish on one hand.

"You know I did! I told you so myself!" Kitty hissed, clearly making a monolith effort to get control of her temper.

9

"I do think I remember you saying something about a party," Lydia conceded, "maybe that's where I got the idea for my shin-dig this Friday."

"You *stole* the idea!" Kitty insisted.

"Kitty darling, be reasonable. You didn't *invent* the idea of parties now, did you? Anyone is free to have a party if they want to. You're perfectly welcome to throw a party still, if you think it could measure up to mine."

Kitty clenched her hands into fists and seemed a beat away from stamping her feet like a child.

"Maybe I *will* still throw a party!" she snapped.

"In your little flower shop? How sweet," Lydia offered, her words dripping with condescension.

Kitty's eyes filled with tears as she flung from the shop, the bell sounding frantically in her wake.

"Between you and me, it's not as though she can even *afford* to throw a party! And it's not as though it would do much good if she did, frumpy little thing like her," Lydia confided, turning back to meet Maggie's stony gaze.

"You should be careful Lydia. You'll push someone too far one of these days," Maggie told her darkly.

"Is that a threat?"

"It's a warning. From one old lady to another."

Lydia smirked, an expression that looked anything but cheerful, and made her way slowly to the door, moving

10

with impossible grace in six inch stiletto heels.

"I'll send Mary round with your formal invitations," she told them graciously, her eyes lingering on Heidi, "but don't feel you have to come."

An unnatural hush descended in her absence, rather as though a tornado had passed through and everyone was surveying the damage.

"Gosh, she's horrible," Shelley managed at last, always temperate.

"Kitty had it right this time dear, that woman is a cow."

Maggie's tone was decisive and her words brought a smile to Shelley's troubled face.

"She was horrid to you! The nerve of her, calling you an old lady!" Shelley remarked crossly.

"I am an old lady!" Maggie cackled, "She didn't like being reminded of her own advanced years though, did she?"

"How old do you think she is?" Shelley asked in a hushed whisper.

"Lydia? She's forty-five if she's a day! *I* know that isn't really old, but she certainly seems to think it is! Colours her hair and dresses like a teenager, but I guarantee she's well past that! She should age gracefully like me," Maggie insisted.

Heidi had retreated back to her spot behind the

counter while the two women spoke, but at least in her own mind, she had to agree. Lydia was all flash and no substance, her look carefully crafted to create the impression of youth and sexuality, while Maggie was something else entirely. Maggie had worked part time in the book shop all Heidi's life, and in that time she didn't seem to have aged, so much as ripened and matured. She was a glittering butterfly bedecked in silks and sparkles. She reminded Heidi of a twenties Hollywood starlet, with a sort of timeless glamour. Anywhere else in the world she might have looked out of place, but in the eccentric beauty of Cross-Town Books, she appeared perfectly at home.

"We are all going to that party!" she announced suddenly, looking from Shelley to Heidi with determination.

Heidi kept her eyes fixed on the ledger in front of her, not betraying by even the flicker of an eyelash that she had heard the older woman's words.

"I see you Heidi Cross! And I tell you now, you are *going* to that party!"

Heidi had become adept at refusing to attend social gatherings, but she had never had to contend with such stubbornness from Maggie before.

"You need to spend time with people," Maggie insisted when she had Heidi cornered that afternoon.

"I spend time with people all day! My job is to serve customers!" Heidi reminded her, working to keep her voice level.

"That's not the same thing and you know it. You need to socialise! To talk to people your own age! To make friends!"

Heidi didn't respond. She had no idea what to say and so defaulted to an uncomfortable silence that just seemed to aggravate Maggie further.

"This is all Joan! Not you!" she cried despairingly.

"Aunt Joan was wonderful," Heidi whispered, her voice small but sure.

Maggie wilted with obvious regret but still looked sad and tired as she gazed at the young woman before her.

"Joan did a good thing, moving in here and raising you. I'm not denying that. She stepped out of her comfort zone and she did her absolute best for you. But maybe it's time you stepped out of your comfort zone too."

It was manipulation and they both knew it. Joan had been gone for almost ten years but she was still, very much a central figure in Heidi's life. Heidi had lost both of her parents in a car accident at the tender age of eight and her only living relative, her father's aunt, had uprooted her own life to care for her and run the bookshop that her parents had loved so much. Joan had been an unconventional guardian, but Heidi had clung to her. She was very much set in her own ways and ideas, but she had also adored her nephew and protected his own views and plans as sacrosanct.

Cross-Town Books looked just as it had when Phillip and Alice had been alive, and their flat above the shop was part living space- part shrine. Joan had kept their memories alive and made sure that their daughter knew exactly who they had been. Weekends had been spent watching their favourite films and listening to their favourite songs. Their favourite books had been read and re-read so many times that the pages were worn soft and pliant. Heidi didn't attend birthday parties or go to the park. She didn't go on shopping trips with friends or have play-dates with other children from school. Joan and Heidi were a team, the two of them sunk deep in their grief, separate from the rest of the world. They were content with their ghosts.

But Joan was gone. Heidi had one more ghost to live with, but it didn't feel the same.

"Alright, I'll think about it," she conceded, earning herself a beaming smile from Maggie. The woman stepped forward to hug her but halted abruptly as Heidi flinched back.

"Sorry-" Heidi began awkwardly.

"Quite alright dear," Maggie assured her with a smile and a nod, stepping back to let Heidi past her.

Joan hadn't been a touchy feely person, and Heidi

had lost the knack of being held.

"I'm not saying for definite-" Heidi added.

"Understood."

Having to be content with that, Heidi made her way back to the counter to regain her post, and settled to hoping that the party would be cancelled. She suspected that that would be the only way that Maggie would let her off the hook.

She hadn't indulged in these thoughts for long before a pale, mousy creature appeared in the doorway, wincing slightly at the chime of the bell.

"Mary!" Maggie called, stepping out from between the shelves with an effusive welcome.

"Hello Maggie," Mary greeted her with a smile.

"You're looking tired, is that woman running you ragged?" Maggie asked sharply, looking over Mary's wan face.

"Two days really isn't long to put this kind of event together," Mary responded diplomatically.

"Ah yes! The party!"

"I have your invitations here," Mary announced, pulling out three envelopes.

Heidi could make out the swirling calligraphy even from across the room. Her heart sank. This event was going to be even more elaborate than she could have imagined.

"Going all out, is she? Hoping to snag herself an investor or a boyfriend?" Maggie enquired.

"I think she'd jump at either," Mary chuckled before catching herself and looking around quickly.

"You're safe, she's not here. You shouldn't have to feel scared of her dear, she's your employer, not your jailer," Maggie counselled.

Mary gave a tight smile that seemed to allow for the possibility of Lydia being both, but refrained from saying anything.

"Are you at least looking forward to the party?" Maggie asked, taking pity.

"I'll be working," Mary told her with a definite frown.

"What?!"

"I'll be serving food and drink. Lydia thinks it wouldn't give the right impression for me to be there like any other guest."

"That's ridiculous!" Maggie cried.

"Well I'm an employee-" Mary began but Maggie, irate, cut her off.

"Mary you should quit! That woman treats you like- like- I don't even know what! Like rubbish! Like the dirt on her shoe! You're planning this party aren't you? You're doing all of the work? But she doesn't even have the decency to let you enjoy it!"

"I don't mind," Mary insisted. "I'll still get to be there at least, and I am her employee. I've worked for Lydia for years! I can't just leave now! It would all be for nothing!"

"What's the alternative dear? Stay with her forever?" Maggie sounded wondering and appalled.

"When she retires I'll take over! The business will finally be mine!" Mary told them, her tone full of desperation and hope.

Heidi felt a twist somewhere in the region of her stomach and turned away quickly, ledger in hand, forcing herself to focus on the words in front of her, safely confined to paper.

Go Set A Watchman.

The Travelling Cat Chronicles.

The Colour Of Magic.

She read the titles, gathering each letter carefully in her mind and making sense of them, drowning out Mary and Maggie completely. She didn't surface again until Mary was gone and Maggie was looking over at her with an unreadable expression.

Heidi lifted one eyebrow defiantly, causing Maggie to shrug and shake her head gently.

"That woman is fooling herself. I'm surrounded by crazy women," she muttered, grabbing a duster and starting to run it over the shelves closest to the window.

It had been a long day and Heidi felt drained. She was regretting agreeing to attend the party and an onslaught of tourists had left her feeling wrung out. With a slow, deep breath, she let herself into her flat and locked the door firmly behind her. The shop downstairs was locked for the day too of course, but the more fastened barriers between her and the world outside, the better.

"I'm home," she called softly.

The blue walls with their painted birds made her feel utterly at peace. A delicately rendered robin watched her slip off her shoes, with a thoughtful expression. The medley of paintings and photographs, hung in frames, tugged at the corners of her lips. Her beautiful, faded pink velvet sofa awaited her, and, sitting in the Queen Anne chair beside it, was Joan.

"A party? Really?"

"I know, I know, but you remember what Maggie's like, she wouldn't let it go!" Heidi argued feebly.

"That woman is an old goat! Though I know she would probably say the same about me," Joan admitted gruffly.

"She just worries."

"She bullies!"

"Maybe she can do both," Heidi suggested fairly.

"Well I don't think you should go. There's no reason

to mix with all the other busy-bodies in the street, we're fine here just as we are," Joan insisted.

"I know we are aunt Joan. Maybe I'll find a way out of it," she murmured vaguely, turning her attention to the kitchen as she wondered what to have for dinner. Heidi usually prepared in advance and had a plan already formed long before she came home, but the drama throughout the day had left her feeling unsettled and knocked her from her usual steady track. As she made the decision to rummage through the fridge looking for inspiration, the elderly woman in the lounge blinked out of existence.

After much internal debate, Heidi decided on pasta and a jar of pasta sauce. It was the best that she could do without running out to get additional ingredients, and she wasn't prepared to brave the public again so soon. She added copious amounts of cheese, to make it feel more like a treat and less like a hastily prepared emergency meal, and vowed to get things back on track tomorrow. The party hadn't even arrived yet and it was already impacting her carefully ordered life. Joan was right about it being a mistake.

She ate her food in front of the telly, curled up with her mother's favourite blanket and her father's favourite film- Indiana Jones. She thought about summoning one of them up to share the evening with her, but she found that actually she was content to be alone. Her figments, as she had started to call them, weren't bringing her quite so much comfort any more. Without Joan to reinforce her memories of her parents, they were becoming hazy and indistinct, softening around the edges. Joan was anything but softened, still clear and crisp as she had been in life, and just as unlikely to provide comfort.

Once the film was over, Heidi retreated to her bedroom. It was painted the same blue as the rest of the flat, a colour that her mother had apparently fallen in love with and bought by the gallon. A small, hand painted blue-tit perched over the light-switch and a flock of blackbirds flitted across one corner and wall of the room. Alice Cross had painted every bird herself, soon after they had moved in, and they were all beautiful. Alice could also be detected in the literature that graced the bookshelf. Whereas Heidi's father had had a penchant for Sci-fi, Alice, like her daughter, had preferred mysteries. There was the odd historical romance in evidence, but primarily the shelves were decked with Agatha Christie and Patricia Wentworth. Most of the clothes had also belonged to Alice before Heidi had discovered them, still snug in the master bedroom's wardrobe when she was just fourteen. At that point everything had been a little too big, a shade too long, but she had persevered. Alice Cross had wonderful style, an eclectic mix of beautiful fifties pieces and more ethereal, almost hippieish clothes. Heidi had endured a few years of looking odd and melancholy before finally her body caught up and she could wear her mother's clothes with easy grace. Each garment fit like a glove and felt like a coat of armour. To sleep however, Heidi preferred her father's things. Her mother's nightgowns were all silky, beautifully embroidered and felt impossibly intimate. Now she pulled on an oversized Star Trek t-shirt, worn and washed so many times that it's design had almost worn away. She teamed it with her father's striped pyjama bottoms and climbed gratefully beneath the covers with a tired and dog-eared copy of Cat Amongst The Pigeons. Before long, sleep overtook her.

Chapter 2

Heidi woke to the comforting smell of paper and found the book still pressed to her cheek. She closed it carefully and settled it back on her beside table before forcing herself out of bed.

"Get everything on track," she muttered to herself, wiping sleep from her eyes.

"That's the spirit dear!" the figment of Joan called from the next room.

She started with water. Ice cold water, in a large glass, condensation running down to her elbow. Next up was yoghurt and fruit, a light breakfast to start the day and give her energy. Joan scoffed at her exercise garb from her spot on the Queen Anne chair, just as she always had, but Heidi didn't care. Her leggings and vest tops were the only clothes she had purchased for herself in years, and it was just one more uniform to don. She made her way down the narrow back stairs, that she only used when she went running, and took a moment to stretch before setting off.

This. This was exactly what she needed. Her routine,

her life, tracking her speed with the running app on her phone. She carefully watched her pace as she followed her usual route, pounding the cobbled streets with her powerful stride. She didn't need to think about anything else, just the ground falling away beneath her as she ran. The world slipped by and her chest heaved. Perfection.

She arrived back at the shop, panting and sweating but with both feet firmly on the ground. She unlocked the back door and took the stairs two at a time, her adrenaline still pumping. After a cool shower she poured herself a large iced coffee and headed downstairs to open the shop. Everything was as it should be.

"Good morning Heidi darling! Are you looking forward to tomorrow?" Maggie sang as she swept in just moments later.

Heidi recognised the question for what it was, a declaration of absolute determination. Maggie had extracted a promise from Heidi and she wasn't going to let it go.

"Tomorrow is a long time away," Heidi countered evenly.

"Not long enough," she added to herself.

They set to work checking the window display, setting up the till and making sure the children's section was clean, organised and ready to go.

"There's something missing here," Maggie

murmured abstractedly and then again louder, "there's something missing!"

"What's that?" Heidi asked nervously.

"The bell is gone!" Maggie exclaimed in distress.

"The bell?!" Heidi asked in alarm, looking instinctively towards the door.

"No, the *old* bell! The one you kept behind the counter!" Maggie clarified, wringing her hands.

Heidi moved swiftly to the counter, her insides chilled.

"The bell from when the shop first opened?" she asked quickly, leaning over to peer behind the counter.

Maggie was right, the spot usually occupied by a small brass bell with no clapper, was now conspicuously empty. When the bell had lost its sound, her father had worked valiantly to repair it but to no avail. Eventually he had found a replacement at a flea market, but he'd kept the old bell behind the desk as a sort of talisman or good-luck charm. Heidi had kept it just where he left it for twenty years and seeing it gone was like a knife to her heart.

"This is unacceptable!" Maggie cried, her dismay quickly turning to fury.

"It's gone," Heidi murmured to herself.

"It's a disgrace! I *know* that bell was there yesterday at closing!"

Heidi didn't manage to say anything at all this time.

Things had been disappearing more and more frequently but this was the first time for something of such emotional significance.

"I suppose we should be glad it wasn't cash this time, but really! This is the outside of enough!" Maggie stormed.

Heidi would much rather have lost cash. Thanks to three separate life insurance policies, money was something she didn't lack, but mementoes of her lost loved ones were of finite supply. She just stared at the desk, her mind blank as she tried not to imagine what her father would say if he knew she had lost the bell. Would he be angry? Sad? Disappointed? She couldn't call an image of him to mind.

"Who could have taken it?!" Maggie demanded to the empty shop.

Heidi couldn't reply. She didn't have any answers and probably couldn't have voiced them if she had.

"What's going on?" a voice asked as the bell over the door trilled.

Heidi tore her eyes away from the desk and turned to face the newcomer with a stricken expression.

"Oh my gosh, what it is?" the woman asked, moving forward hurriedly.

"Another theft, Rose!" Maggie cried, gesturing to the desk before her.

"You're kidding!" Rose exclaimed, stopping in her tracks.

Heidi took the opportunity while she could, slipping away to hide amongst the shelves. She wished that Maggie had kept it a secret. The loss of the bell felt too personal to share, and Heidi didn't want to get drawn into the crusade of the rest of the street, desperate to find the thief who plagued them. She ducked down, behind the shelf on travel books, and listened as Rose and Maggie discussed this latest occurrence.

"We had over a hundred pounds taken last week! I don't know how they're getting in! I know I locked up at the end of the day!" Rose told Maggie.

"We locked up here too dear! You know how careful Heidi is!"

"What was taken? Not more money?" Rose asked anxiously.

"No, it was a bell from behind the desk. Not valuable, but Heidi's father bought it so she's bound to be upset," Maggie explained.

"It's awful having *anything* taken!"

"It's horrible just to think of someone being here, sitting at the desk, poking around at night. It gives me the creeps! And I hate to think of poor Heidi all alone upstairs!" Maggie said darkly.

"You should tell the police. We're supposed to update them every time something is taken," Rose told her.

"A lot of good it's doing! It seems as though every

business in the street is suffering the same, and the police haven't done a damn thing about it!"

Heidi slunk away rather than listen to any more. She liked Rose, she seemed like a sweet girl, but she was Lydia's daughter which meant that they were bound to discuss the party. She ended up spending most of the day ducking behind shelves and darting around corners. She even volunteered to run out for iced coffees twice during the afternoon, just to avoid the sporadic appearances by neighbours looking to discuss potential outfits with Maggie and Shelley. She couldn't blame them, the party was occupying her thoughts too, just in a very different way. Heidi was mentally practising small talk rather than planning her ensemble. She only owned one dress that would be suitable for the occasion and really, the chance to wear it was this events only saving grace. Heidi had worn everything else in her mother's wardrobe but this one item hadn't had a showing since Alice had last worn it. When anxiety threatened to take hold, Heidi pictured the dress in her mind's eye and reminded herself that she didn't have to stay long.

She made it through the day like this and rewarded herself with one of her favourite evening routines. She put Gilmore Girls on the television, a show that her mother had loved and her father had groaningly endured. Heidi had vivid recollections of watching episodes with her mother, laughing when she laughed and eating Pop-Tarts in solidarity with Rory. She made herself a batch of macaroni cheese, from scratch of course, and dished herself up a serving with a side salad of mixed greens tossed in a balsamic glaze. She let Lorelai's voice soothe her from the living room as she stirred and grated, before finally settling down to watch in earnest with her plate of food.

"I love this one," her mother commented from her seat on the sofa beside her.

"I know," Heidi agreed with a small smile.

"We had so much fun watching this."

Heidi nodded, smothering a small pang at her mother's use of the past tense.

She returned her focus to her food as the image of Alice faded away. She let herself sink into the comfort of familiar storylines and predictable dialogue. This. This was the right way to spend an evening.

She pushed the thoughts down, letting herself forget about the outside world for the time-being. She remained in her safe, secluded bubble until morning, following her routines with practised ease.

When she woke she felt better. It took a few minutes for her to remember that it was the day of party, and even then she had set jobs to distract her for a while.

She started the day with a run again, coming very close to her personal best despite the heat already setting in. She dressed, brushed out her hair and poured her iced coffee into her waiting cup. She unlocked the shop and set about dusting, checking as she went for any other missing items. Everything seemed to be in place. She let out a sigh of relief as she arrived at last at the cash desk and found everything except the bell, waiting exactly where it should be.

"Any more thefts?!" Maggie demanded from the doorway, striking a dramatic pose.

"No, everything looks fine."

"Well we still need to update the police! And we need to meet with the other shop owners. We have to get to the bottom of this!" Maggie insisted, sweeping across the shop, her sequinned wrap throwing spots of light across the room.

"I'll call the police this afternoon," Heidi agreed, carefully side-stepping the rest of Maggie's speech.

"And you're going to the party this evening?" Maggie demanded, her eyes narrowed with suspicion.

"Yes, at least for a bit," Heidi agreed with a sigh.

"Good. You deserve to meet the eligible Mr Bingley as much as anyone else does. You've been alone too long."

Heidi almost smiled at this. Not so much at Maggie's desire to set her up, but at the comfortable assumption that Mr Bingley would be open to it. No one in the street seemed to have considered the possibility that Mr Bingley wasn't looking for a wife or a girlfriend, but rather just wanted to successfully launch his shop.

"Matt's mum agreed to keep Imogen overnight!" Shelley called happily over the chime of the door.

"Wonderful! No Cinderella act for you my girl, you can dance until dawn!" Maggie crowed delightedly.

"I don't know about that," Shelley chuckled, blushing but obviously excited.

Heidi wasn't sure how old Shelley was, but she thought that she might be a similar age to herself. It seemed impossible that she had an ex-husband and a daughter in that time, but her smooth, freckled skin and bright blue eyes wouldn't allow for her being much older.

"What are you going to wear?" Maggie asked excitedly.

"A black dress I wore for my last anniversary with Matt. You don't think that's bad luck, do you?"

"Of course not! Besides, determination is far more powerful than luck! Everyone knows that! What about you Heidi, do you know what you're wearing this evening?"

Heidi saw Shelley's eyes widen in surprise but her smile looked genuine.

"You're coming?" she asked.

Heidi gave a small half shrug with a portion of nod thrown in.

"I have an old dress of my mother's."

"Alice had such wonderful clothes, and you wear them beautifully," Maggie told her sincerely.

Heidi smiled despite herself but quickly retreated to the back of the shop with a duster and a can of polish. Over the course of the day they received another visit from Rose, this time with cakes fresh from the bakery for them all, a visit from Kitty, one from Jane and Elizabeth at the dress shop, and even a visit from Mr Price who owned the model plane shop. Heidi suspected that more of their neighbours stopped in, but by mid afternoon she was firmly ensconced in a back corner with an audio book, so only Maggie and Shelley could say for sure.

"Alright, off with you."

Heidi looked up in surprise, removing her earbuds. "Sorry?"

"Go, on. Upstairs. I'll lock up the shop, but you make sure you're back down here at eight because I'm going to be here waiting to walk over to the party with you," Maggie told her firmly.

"That's alright, it's only just gone four, it isn't time yet-" Heidi began in protest.

"Heidi dear, there's no sense you staying down here, tucked away, getting yourself more and more anxious. Parties are supposed to be fun! Now go upstairs and find something to distract yourself with for a few hours. I'll be back here to get you at eight on the dot."

After just a moments hesitation, Heidi agreed and clambered to her feet. It was almost unheard of for her to leave work early- once wouldn't hurt. She was the boss after all!

"Thank you Maggie," she muttered gratefully as she passed.

Fleeing upstairs, she let out a deep breath when she gained the solitude of her flat. It was good to be alone, even with the spectre of Joan watching her with a decided frown.

"It's one party!" she hissed.

"It's nonsense is what it is!" Joan barked, "And worse, it's that ghastly woman!"

Heidi sighed at this. She did wish that it wasn't Lydia. The woman was a bully and she managed to set everyone on edge wherever she went. It would be hard to avoid her at her own party, but Heidi vowed to do her best.

"I think it sounds lovely," Alice murmured softly, from the door of the bedroom.

Heidi smiled sadly. Her mother was fading with time, losing her vibrancy, but she was still the voice that countered Joan. She urged patience and kindness. Heidi allowed herself to wonder what her mother would really have said, how she would really have looked and sounded. Joan was so vivid and real still, but Alice was just a shade- the haze of memories gathered together into a form gleaned more from photographs than recollections at this point.

"It's going to be nice," Heidi agreed, silencing Joan with a single look, "and in the mean time I'm going to get some knitting done and watch something to get me in a party mood."

She opted for Dirty Dancing followed by Jumanji, figuring that she had all her bases covered that way. She kept dinner light, dishing herself out a small bowl of leftover mac'n'cheese from the fridge. The party was supposed to have food, but she didn't know what that would entail and she didn't want to arrive hungry. She tended to be an early eater, since that had always been Joan's preference.

Finally, she could put it off no longer, she would have to get ready and change into her outfit. She started with hair and make-up, keeping it simple. Her hair was long and dark, just like her mother's, and she decided to wear it down. She'd never got the hang of curling or styling it, but the length and colour made it look beautiful anyway. Make-up was something that Joan had never shown any inclination toward, and her mother had died while Heidi was still too young to really have much of an interest in such things. She'd picked up a little knowledge through osmosis, but she always kept things simple. Mascara, blush, lip tint, and maybe even a little eyeliner if she was feeling particularly ambitious. The memory of her mother watched with approval, though she didn't offer any advice. All in all, Heidi wasn't dissatisfied with the result, though she knew she would likely pale in comparison to the artistry other people seemed to engage in with a make-up brush. No contouring or highlighting for her, she acknowledged with a small sigh.

She stepped into the dress and pulled it up around her, sliding the zip up the back with ease. It was a thrill every time her mother's clothes went on. Each morning, when they fitted her form, she felt a spark of joy. She couldn't remember Alice with the clarity she longed for, but she could step out into the world in her clothes, and that was something. She stepped into the matching heels and observed the effect in the mirror. It was perfect. It was worth attending a party for this.

The dress was off white, patterned all over with beading, a subtle twenties style. Not quite a flapper dress but leaning that way. The shoes were the same off-white, with almost three inches of heel, raising Heidi up to a whopping five foot six.

"You look beautiful," Alice whispered.

"I look like you," Heidi agreed with a smile.

She had pictures of her mother wearing this outfit. If she stepped back and squinted, she could almost believe it was Alice in the mirror now. That same hair, the same shape and height, just the set of the features and the colour of the eyes not quite a match for the real thing. Alice's features had been strong, sharp, perfect. Heidi was a little more indistinct. Her father's genes had muddied the water just enough to make her a plain imitation of her mother. She didn't mind though, she wouldn't want Alice's striking, attention-grabbing beauty. She liked to see her father's soft nose, small mouth and kind blue eyes looking out of her face. She wasn't a perfect copy of either one of them but she did her absolute best to be both.

Chapter 3

"Beautiful," Alice said again, still smiling at her daughter.

"I suppose I better head down, or Maggie will be storming up here to find me," Heidi commented, seeing the time.

Really it was only just gone ten to eight, but it wasn't in Heidi's nature to be late. She was grateful for those extra minutes when it came to walking down the stairs in her mother's heels.

"You look beautiful, Heidi," Maggie told her sincerely.

"Oh Heidi you look wonderful!" Shelley exclaimed, queueing Heidi to blush and push her hair behind her ears.

"You look great Shelley," Heidi offered.

It was true, Shelley was in a black dress with lace detailing. Her skin looked starkly pale in comparison but it was an eye-catching effect that highlighted her slim legs and arms.

"And Maggie, you look amazing as always," Heidi added, admiring Maggie's green satin dress and black sequinned shrug.

"I've always known how to dress for a party," Maggie agreed happily.

"We should get going I suppose, the music is already playing and I could see people arriving as we passed," Shelley told them, her cheeks already flushed with excitement.

Heidi agreed, doing her best to ignore the churning of her stomach. They walked slowly, giving Heidi a little extra time to get used to her heels and to slow her breathing.

"Gosh, I'm not used to these shoes! My feet are already killing me!" Shelley exclaimed, though Heidi wasn't sure whether it was solely for her benefit.

"Well they're worth it dear. You both look ravishing in such exquisite footwear," Maggie insisted, gesturing to both of their heels.

Heidi didn't say anything. The music was getting louder, swelling to fill the street, and she could already make out laughter and the chink of glasses, even before they reached Luscious Whisper, Lydia's lingerie shop.

"Luscious Whisper," Heidi muttered to herself under her breath, as she did every time she passed the shop.

Maggie snorted with laughter and Heidi felt herself smiling.

"Garish, isn't it."

Heidi gave a half nod of agreement and Shelley giggled.

"One thing I will say, the woman knows how to throw a party," Maggie admitted, stopping briefly in her tracks.

Luscious Whisper had been designed as both an event space and shop, mostly catering to hen dos and the odd birthday party. This evening however, it had been fully opened up and stock had been hidden away in store rooms, leaving a large space for dancing, drinking, mingling and socialising, with just the products hanging from the walls to make Heidi blush and feel uncomfortable. She averted her gaze from something lacy and frilly as they made their way inside and looked about them.

"Heidi! You came!" Lydia sing-songed, instantly upon them.

"You invited me," she responded, cringing at the irritation at the edge of Lydia's words.

"Gosh! It's just so strange to see you somewhere like this! You're such a mouse, I-"

"We're getting drinks," Maggie cut in, pushing past Lydia and making her totter in impossibly high stiletto heels.

Shelley and Heidi followed in Maggie's wake, shuffling quickly to keep up with her. The shop was busy, crowded with neighbours and people that Heidi was sure she didn't recognise.

"Who are all these guests?!" she exclaimed in a slight panic.

"People's friends and family, Lydia's friends, who knows?" Shelley replied comfortably, looking around as though completely unphased.

"I don't even *know* this many people," Heidi muttered, completely unnecessarily.

Heidi was a hermit. That really didn't involve a lot of socialising.

"I don't think much of the music, but this is great!" Shelley commented as they reached a cash desk that had been converted into a bar.

"Three glasses of fizzy please dear," Maggie requested of the young man serving. He quickly obliged, evidently relieved that they hadn't requested cocktails.

"Here you are ladies!"

He handed the three glasses over with a smile.

"Aren't you Robert?" Shelley asked, scrutinising him.

"Yep, that's me!" he agreed.

"Rose's young man?" Maggie chimed in.

"The very same."

He was still smiling, though looking a little wary now.

"Why are you working here? I thought you had a job in marketing," Maggie challenged.

"He does! But he's crazy!" A voice called over them, making Heidi turn quickly.

For a second she thought it was Lydia, but it was Rose approaching behind them.

"She asked me to help! What was I supposed to say?!" he asked her, hand on hip.

"Considering she treats you like crap and doesn't even want us dating, you say *no*!"

"I need to get her to like me! You know I do!" he retorted, slight desperation creeping into his voice.

"This isn't going to help," she told him sadly, stepping behind the bar and kissing him on the cheek.

It wasn't a particularly intimate moment but Heidi instinctively turned her gaze away.

"Oh Heidi! Such a prude!" Lydia cackled, appearing suddenly and wrapping an arm around Heidi's shoulders, making her squirm.

"Mum!" Rose exclaimed, reaching up quickly to put a hand on Robert's arm.

"Rose, darling, it looks a bit odd you standing behind the bar there, almost as though you're the help!" Lydia chuckled.

"What?" Rose asked in a cold voice.

"I just think people prefer to know their place darling, I don't mean any offence! Robert knows that, don't you Robert?" Lydia crooned, throwing Robert a look

40

of complete innocence.

"Oh! Yeah! I guess I'm not offended," he stammered quickly.

Rose took a step back, her eyes flashing.

"*Not offended?* You prefer to *know your place?*" she demanded her eyes flashing.

He blustered hopelessly as Lydia watched, smiling.

"I hired Robert for the evening. I am paying for his services. But you're my daughter, if you stand behind the bar it muddies the social waters, don't you think?" Lydia asked sweetly.

"Is that why you're making Mary work this evening?" Rose snapped, switching her focus immediately back to her mother.

"She's my staff. Of course she's working," Lydia replied, seemingly mystified by the question.

"She's worked for you for years! She's practically a partner in the business!"

"Practically isn't actually!" Lydia sang, setting Heidi's teeth on edge.

Lydia still had her arm around Heidi, her skin sticky across Heidi's shoulders and the intense scent of her perfume clogging Heidi's nostrils. The music was starting to shake inside her bones and she could feel her eyelids closing against the flashing of the lights.

"Heidi! Let's go to the bathroom!" Shelley cried

suddenly, reaching out and pulling her from Lydia's grip.

"Back in a sec!" Shelley called over her shoulder with a smile and a wave as she led Heidi by the hand through the crowd.

Heidi focussed on her breathing. In for three, out for four. Three and four were both good numbers. Three was half of six and four was two twos. Two and six were both *great* numbers, but too short and too long for breathing.

"Let's just cool down for a moment," Shelley suggested.

Heidi gathered herself enough to realise that they weren't headed for the bathroom, they were actually making their way outside. She breathed a sigh of relief and quickened her steps a little.

"That sounds good," she murmured, forcing the words out.

"It's so hot in there!"

They had finally reached the street and Shelley gave a little shake, casting off the closeness of the party.

"So hot," Heidi agreed feebly.

"I haven't been to a party in ages!"

"No, me neither," Heidi agreed, wishing she could think of something more substantial to say. She was fully aware that Shelley had just saved her and whisked her away in an act of charity, but the last party she had been to was Bethany Staple's eighth birthday party twenty years before and she was feeling decidedly out of practice.

"Lydia is a nightmare, isn't she," Shelley commented, seemingly unruffled by Heidi's conversational shortcomings.

"Poor Rose," Heidi nodded, silently congratulating herself on offering some actual input.

"And poor Robert too! They want to get married but Lydia's making things difficult. Robert's still new at his job and Lydia's made it clear that she's going to cut Rose off if they go through with a wedding. How she can judge poor Robert, after everything I heard about her ex-husband, is a mystery," Shelley finished with a huff.

"Not a good guy?" Heidi surmised.

"Apparently a bit of a rogue, as Maggie would say. Always borrowing money and not paying it back, trying to scam people, that sort of thing."

Heidi mulled this over, once again lost for words. She liked Rose, from a distance, and it seemed impossible that the sweet young woman had come from two such unpleasant parents.

"Robert seems nice though," she eventually offered, earning herself a nod of agreement from Shelley.

"Yeah, he seems lovely and Rose obviously adores him. I just hope Lydia doesn't manage to tear them apart. She doesn't seem to set much store by engagements, or by other people's relationships at all really."

They relapsed into silence for a few minutes, sipping on their wine and making the most of the slight breeze, before Shelley checked the time.

"We should probably head back in. You ready?"

Heidi agreed, though she would much rather have fled back across the street to the peace and safety of her home. They got top-ups on their wine and then set about wending their way through the crowd in search of Maggie. They found her looking decidedly cosy with Mr Price, a theatrical man who always spoke as though he were quoting Shakespeare. Heidi paused, wondering whether they should slip away again and leave them to it, but Maggie spotted them and waved them over.

"Girls! There you are! Alexander was just telling me that they had another break in last week!" she reported excitedly.

"Really?" Heidi asked, her interest piqued.

Mr Price, or *Alexander* apparently, gave a slight bow as confirmation.

"Was much taken?" Shelley enquired.

"Some money," he replied with a shrug.

Heidi was longing to ask how he could afford to be so blasé about it. Model planes were such an incongruous item, and she never saw people going into the shop, so she couldn't understand how he stayed afloat, even without having money stolen. She supposed that like her, he must own the shop outright and not have rent payments to worry about.

"The police are useless!" Maggie exclaimed furiously.

"They are indeed, dear lady. I reported the latest happening to them and they did nothing more than write it down."

"They should be investigating! They should be checking CCTV! Questioning people!"

"Most burglaries go unsolved. For the most part, the police don't have the resources to investigate them, and the chances of stolen money or goods being recovered is very low," Heidi rattled off. She'd been researching the statistics since the bell was stolen, trying and failing to reassure herself that it could be found.

"Who do you believe they should be questioning?" Mr Price asked, spreading his hands wide as though to show that he didn't have any potential suspects secreted about his person.

"I don't know, local vagabonds?" Maggie suggested vaguely.

"I'm not sure I know of any local vagabonds, but CCTV should be an option, shouldn't it?" Shelley asked.

"There aren't exactly cameras on every corner," Heidi commented with a shrug, "And there's no cash point on this street, so there's no camera there to access."

"Someone needs to get security cameras in their

shop," Shelley suggested brightly.

"Catch them in the act!" Maggie added.

"I'm afraid I couldn't afford something like that," Mr Price admitted, a flush creeping up his neck, "But perhaps the ladies at the clothing shop? Or in the florist? I hear they have more reason than most to want this taken care of."

"What do you mean? What's been stolen from them?!" Maggie demanded.

"Not theft dear lady, blackmail!"

His words were met with silence and all three women slowly digested their meaning.

"B-blackmail?" Shelley eventually stammered in disbelief.

"I know! It seems inconceivable in our little Cross Street community, doesn't it," he commented, his slightly theatrical sorrow starting to grate on Heidi's nerves.

"But how are they being blackmailed?! What about?!" Maggie asked.

"As to how, I believe notes were left, with instructions to leave money and valuables for the blackmailer to take. As to what..." he trailed off, his hands open wide, his palms upturned as he shrugged.

"Elizabeth, Jane and Kitty? I can't even imagine!" Shelley exclaimed.

"What are we talking about?" Kitty's voice sounded,

causing them all to turn quickly, their faces in various hues of red, scarlet and pink.

"Oh there you are dear! We were just wondering if you were here!" Maggie rushed to explain, her voice just a little too loud and high to be entirely natural.

"Of course I'm here! I wasn't going to let a little misunderstanding with Lydia keep me from welcoming Mr Bingley and Mr Darcy here to the street!" Kitty responded firmly, drawing the two men with her into the conversation.

"Darcy? I thought it was Darby," Shelley whispered to Heidi.

"Oh Mr Bingley! So lovely to see you!" Maggie gushed, keen to cover her discomfort "and Mr Darcy! You must be the business partner we've heard tell of!"

"It seems there's no one on this street who *hasn't* heard of me," Mr Darcy agreed with a sneer.

"Well we all know each other, it's a community," Shelley told him anxiously, aware of having committed some kind of faux pas.

"Who would have thought. Small town charm, right in the heart of Cambridge," he scoffed.

A look of amusement was thrown towards Charles Bingley but it was entirely lost on him. His gaze was fixed across the room on Jane and there wasn't an ounce of condescension in his expression.

"You don't approve of community?" Maggie challenged.

"I rather prioritise society."

With this cutting remark, he stalked away through the crowd in the general direction of the bar. No one was particularly sad to see him go, and Maggie watched his departure with particularly close attention.

"Lydia wont have any luck with him," she commented, allowing herself a wry smile.

"I don't know why she'd want to!" Shelley remarked before turning quickly to Mr Bingley, an apology on her lips.

"Don't worry," he chuckled, "Fitz has always made a terrible first impression. He doesn't make a great second impression either to be honest. But we've known each other since our university days and he's always been a good friend. Besides, he knows the business world inside and out! I couldn't have started Apothocary's without him!"

"What made you want to get into gin? Jane asked, stepping over to their group and joining in the conversation with ease.

"Yes! It sounds fascinating!" Kitty added a little too enthusiastically.

"Well it's just such a versatile drink! So many possibilities for flavours and different combinations to try out! Besides, who doesn't love a good G&T at the end of the day?" he responded lightly.

They all laughed politely and quizzed him on his plans for the shop and upcoming flavours of gin that he would be releasing, but it was clear even then that the lions share of his attention was going to Jane. Heidi watched happily, content to soak up the conversation while playing little part in it herself. She enjoyed watching the social ballet enacted before her. Charles would advance and Jane respond, the two taking centre stage as the rest vied for the limelight. Shelley and Maggie were quick to adjust, stepping back to let the two get to know one another, while Kitty was clearly finding it harder to let go.

"You'll have to let me cook for you!" she burst out suddenly, when the topic of food came up.

"Gosh! How *domestic*!" a harsh voice crooned.

Heidi flinched, shrinking slightly even before Lydia slipped into the group.

Kitty turned purple.

"I wasn't talking to you," she spat, clutching her wine glass so tight that her fingers were going white.

"Kitty darling, I could hear you from across the room! That's hardly *my* fault," Lydia, told her, widening her eyes in mock innocence.

If possible, Kitty flushed even darker.

"There you are Charles! I was wondering where you'd hidden yourself! Charming the locals are you?" Lydia enquired laughingly.

Somehow the word 'locals', sounded an awful lot like 'provincials' and Charles squirmed a little, unsure of how to respond.

"Kitty was just kind enough to invite me-" he began before Lydia cut him off.

"Oh I heard that! A dinner invitation! Careful Kitty, you don't want people to think you're trying to take advantage of our dear Mr Bingley, not everyone drinks as much as you do dear."

At Lydia's words there was a crash, followed by a small scream and the tinkle of broken glass. Kitty had inadvertently crushed the wine glass in her hand and blood dripped from her palm.

"Another careless accident?" Lydia asked coldly, "you'll want to go and get yourself cleaned up."

Shelley swept Kitty away towards the bathrooms while the rest of them watched Lydia in fascinated horror.

"What was that?!" Maggie demanded.

"What?" Lydia replied, all innocence.

"You shouldn't say things like that about people!" Jane hissed, her expression dark with anger.

"You think I should be protecting people's secrets? Why? They always come out in the end," Lydia told them, her words dripping with disdain.

"You're going to get yourself into trouble," Jane

warned.

"Well you'd know all about that, wouldn't you."

"What's that supposed to mean?!" Jane demanded, her voice rising.

"*I'm* not the one getting letters. No one has anything to hold over *me*," Lydia told her loftily, making Jane turn on the spot and hurry away, her eyes shining with tears.

"It's always the quiet ones," Lydia commented sadly, watching her go, "but really Charles, it was a wonderful idea. I tell you what, *I'll* make you dinner! One evening next week? It would be nice to give you a more... intimate welcome."

Before he could respond to this brightly offered suggestion, a figure stepped up behind him and Lydia's face changed.

"You." she muttered simply.

"Lydia-"

"Lydia Wickes," she confirmed, holding out one red taloned hand for Fitz Darcy to shake.

He didn't take it.

"Lydia Wickes."

"This is my shop," she told him brightly, smoothly retracting her hand and gesturing around them.

"So we have you to thank for this spectacle, do we?"

Heidi had heard enough. She slipped away as quietly as she could, making her way back across the street with her thoughts in a whirl.

Thefts? Blackmail? Drinking? Conniving? Competing for attention?

Joan was right, parties and socialising weren't worth the effort they entailed.

"I told you," Joan croaked, as Heidi let herself in to the flat.

"I know, I know," Heidi muttered, stepping out of her shoes and flexing her toes with satisfaction.

"Not all you hoped?" her mother asked sympathetically, leaning against the bedroom door frame and watching Heidi with concern.

"Not all I hoped. People are awful!" she exclaimed, feeling only a slight twinge of guilt at the generalisation. Maggie wasn't awful, and neither was Shelley. Charles and Jane and Rose and Robert had all been nice, but Fitz Darcy and Lydia had overshadowed them all.

"I told you!" Joan repeated, causing a sharp stab of pain just above Heidi's left eye.

"I know! But I promised Maggie!" she snapped defensively, pressing her fingers to the bridge of her nose and forcing herself to breathe slowly and deeply.

"I just want to go to bed. I want to be alone," she muttered.

When she lowered her hand and opened her eyes, Joan and Alice were both gone. She breathed a small sigh of relief. After removing her make-up and fetching herself some water, she climbed into bed and did her best to ignore the sound of music still drifting across the street from Lydia's shop.

There was so much tension and angst that she hadn't been aware of. She'd been watching her neighbours for years and she wouldn't have believed that there was so much going on beneath the surface. As she listened to the pounding base line of some garish song, she wondered what Elizabeth, Jane or Kitty could possibly have done, to be blackmailed about. They all seemed like nice, normal women, what secrets could they possibly have worth extorting?!

One song after another boomed out, invading Heidi's mind and disrupting her thoughts. It was gone two in the morning before she finally drifted off, and even then her dreams were a tangled mass of music, dancing and a loud, cruel laugh.

Chapter 4

Heidi woke early- even earlier than usual. She knew that she should use the time for an extra long run, but she couldn't bring herself to crawl out of bed just yet. She hadn't gotten any reading done the night before, too distracted by the party and the drama to concentrate on fiction, but she was re-reading her favourite Jane Austen and she wanted a little time in that world before having to rejoin the real one. Snuggling back down under her covers, she delved in. After almost an hour she felt lighter and happier and ready to meet the challenges of the day. She knew that everyone would be buzzing about the party and gossiping about everything that had taken place, but she resolved to remain detached. She would watch events unfold, with the appreciation of a reader consuming a novel.

She dressed simply, in one of her mother's long, floaty summer dresses, and pulled her hair back into a plait. She fetched her iced coffee from the fridge, transferring it to her travel cup, and sipped it happily as she made her way downstairs to the shop. It was still a little too early to open, but she could get a jump on some admin and make sure that she was feeling confident and in control before people started stopping in and customers began arriving. She unlocked the door at the bottom of the stairs and pushed it open, stopping in her tracks.

Lydia.

She was quite possibly the last person that Heidi had expected to see, especially lying in the middle of the floor with a knife sticking out of her back.

"Lydia?" she called feebly, her voice unbelievably small and wavering.

She took a small step forward on legs that felt suddenly numb, and then another and another.

"Lydia?" she tried again, her voice croaking this time, as though she were forcing the words out against their will.

She stopped just short of the figure on the floor and then crouched down, reaching forward with her free hand. She touched Lydia's arm. It felt cold.

Rising quickly, she almost stumbled as she backed away. She needed to do something. Her brain was screaming at her that Lydia was dead and she needed to *do something about it*, but for an agonisingly long moment she couldn't for the life of her think *what*.

Call the police.

The answer sprang to her mind fully formed. She

needed to call the police and tell them that Lydia was dead. She went to the reception desk and fumbled for a second with the phone as her fingers seemed to be infected with the same numbness as her legs.

"What is the nature of the emergency?" a voice asked from a million miles away.

Heidi forced herself to breathe and press the phone to her ear, her gaze still fixed on Lydia's prone form.

"There's a body on the floor," she managed, the words bursting forth in a rush.

"I'm sorry?" the voice queried calmly,

"Someone's dead. Lydia. Lydia is dead. On the floor in my shop," Heidi tried to explain.

"A medical emergency? Have you checked for a pulse?" the voice asked, still utterly calm in the face of Heidi's rambling panic.

"She's cold to the touch. That means she's dead, right? And there's a knife sticking out of her back."

The emergency services operator was truly fantastic. She talked Heidi through checking for a pulse without disturbing or moving Lydia more than was absolutely necessary, and then she instructed her to step out the front of the shop and wait for police who were already en route.

"I can't believe this is happening," Heidi mumbled, cringing at the cliché.

"I understand, don't worry, the police will be there

soon and I can stay on the line with you until they arrive."

"No, no it's alright. Someone is here, someone just arrived, a friend."

Heidi stumbled a little over the word, not sure that it applied, though the sight of Maggie's bright, smiling face had caused her stomach to flip and made her eyes flood with tears.

"Hello dear! What are you doing out here?!" Maggie called as she approached, watching Heidi curiously.

"We can't go in," Heidi told her, blinking furiously.

"Can't go in?"

"There's a body on the floor."

Maggie's expression didn't change, but a flash of uncertainty entered her eyes.

"I'm not sure I follow," she nudged when Heidi didn't elaborate.

"The police are on their way. I called them when I found the body."

Maggie darted a look at the closed door and then back at Heidi. As she studied the young woman's face she seemed to realise that something terrible really had happened.

"Who?" she asked quickly, her voice a hoarse whisper.

"Lydia."

Heidi detected the faintest of sighs, just a touch of

relief, before the full weight of the situation settled in.

"What's she doing here?" she asked.

"I have no idea! Getting stabbed I suppose," Heidi replied vaguely, her voice sounding unnatural even to her own ears.

"And the police are on their way?" Maggie asked, her eyes narrowing as she observed Heidi.

"Yes, they should be here any minute."

"I think I'll take that then," Maggie announced, reaching out and taking the travel cup still clutched in Heidi's hand.

"Why?" Heidi asked, feeling strangely bereft without it.

"Because the police don't know you like I do dear. If they arrive and you're talking calmly about stabbings and sipping on your iced coffee, they may think you're..." Maggie trailed off, not sure how to finish the thought.

"A suspect?" Heidi offered.

"A sociopath," Maggie countered.

Heidi bristled.

"I'm just an introvert," she grumbled, eliciting a bark of laughter from Maggie.

"Now you've got *me* doing it!" she chastened, pressing a hand to her mouth to block any more inappropriate amusement from escaping.

"Heidi Cross?" a voice called.

Both women turned, with remarkably solemn expressions, to meet the arriving police detective.

"That's me," Heidi told him gravely.

"I'm DS Elliot."

"I'm Maggie Elcott, with two Ts," Maggie chimed in, her face grim.

DS Elliot looked from one dark, formal face to another and started to wonder whether this was some kind of ill advised prank.

"We were told there was a body," he reported doubtfully.

"Yes. It's in there," Heidi told him, gesturing to the shop behind her.

"Cross-Town Books?"

"It's my shop. It's not my body though! Obviously," she trailed off.

"You work here?" he asked, tactfully ignoring her slip.

"I own it. It was my parents' shop," she explained simply, forcing herself to leave it there rather than rambling on.

"Heidi's a good girl," Maggie offered out of the blue, making Heidi cringe slightly. No one was questioning that yet!

"Alright," DS Elliot replied uncertainly, giving Heidi a slightly confused look.

"Well she is! It's not *her* fault there's a body in the bookshop!" Maggie retorted.

DS Elliot was becoming exasperated and made the executive decision to enter the premises and check whether there was indeed a body, or whether the two women outside were just totally and utterly mad. He left Maggie and Heidi in the street, with firm instructions not to move, and headed in. He'd only been gone a couple of minutes when he returned, looking pale and slightly shaken but still admirably collected.

"Do you know the identity of the victim?" he asked them, drawing an involuntary gasp from Maggie.

"Sorry," she muttered, "it's just... victim."

"It's Lydia. Lydia Wickes," Heidi cut in.

"Lydia Wickes. And did you see what happened?" DS Elliot asked, turning his attention to Heidi.

"I have no idea, I didn't see a thing. I just found her there, like that, when I came down to open the shop! She was just... dead."

He studied her face closely, but apparently he was satisfied with her answer because he just made a note of it and carried on.

"What was she doing here?" he asked.

"I have no idea."

Less satisfied.

"What do you mean? Why was she in your shop?

Does she work here? Are you friends?" he fired off the questions one after another, not leaving time for Heidi to think about her answers.

"I have no clue! I don't even know how she got in! She doesn't work here, we're not friends, I don't like her," Heidi reported in a rush.

"Well they weren't *close*," Maggie cut in quickly.

"Sorry?" DS Elliot swung towards Maggie now, notebook and pen poised at the ready.

"Heidi and Lydia weren't *close*, but they weren't enemies or anything! She didn't *dis*like her! Did you Heidi?" She insisted in a voice that brooked no argument.

"Oh! Oh no! Of course not! We just weren't- weren't close. That's all."

DS Elliot looked at them both, obviously unimpressed.

"I've only been here two minutes, I'm not trying to trick you! Can you just answer the questions? I need to know as much as possible to find out what happened here," he told them sincerely, knocking both women off their guard.

"Oh," Maggie stammered, "Yes, sorry, I was just..."

"Lydia owns the lingerie shop further down the street. We're neighbours. She threw a party last night, that's the last time I saw her. I really don't know what she's doing here in the shop," Heidi explained apologetically.

"Thank you. Who else was at this party?"

"The whole street, I think. Oh dear! Rose!" Maggie exclaimed, putting a hand to her mouth and looking at them both, wide eyed.

"Rose?"

"Her daughter! Someone will have to tell her!" Maggie looked distraught at the thought of it.

"Don't worry, we'll handle that. Do you know how we can reach her?" DS Elliot asked soothingly.

"She works at the bakery! She might even be there now! What if she sees?!"

Maggie was clearly not going to be soothed. The arrival of more uniformed officers on the scene did nothing to calm her. DS Elliot guided them a little further away as the scene was secured but Maggie was watching the goings on in a panic.

"What if Rose sees all this?! What if she comes over! She can't find out in the street like that!"

Eventually DS Elliot conceded, allowing Maggie and Heidi to walk him to the bakery so that he could try to find Rose immediately and break the news before the police presence and crime scene tape did it for him.

"You two wait out here please," DS Elliot requested, before going inside alone.

Maggie and Heidi had no desire to go with him, preferring to huddle outside in the street and peer awkwardly through the bakery window. DS Elliot was met at the kitchen door by a smiling Rose. Heidi watched as her face went slack, losing all expression. She stepped back, looking away before Rose crumpled. She didn't want to be this close to that kind of grief.

She pulled in a deep breath, holding it for three, then out for four. Three and four. Good numbers.

"I want to go back to the shop and see what's happening," she told Maggie, already backing away.

"I'm not sure we're allowed to go anywhere, the Detective said to stay put."

"I won't go far, I'll stay in the street, near the bookshop, I just- I want to keep an eye on things. You can tell DS Elliot where I am."

"You don't want me to come with you?" Maggie asked, reaching out a tentative hand.

"No, no, it's fine. I just want to stay near the bookshop," Heidi told her, but she kept her eyes fixed on the bakery as though it were an approaching predator that might strike at any moment.

"Alright dear, I'll tell him where to find you."

That was all she needed, Heidi ran. She was back across the street in seconds, fleeing along the pavement, putting one step after another between her and Rose.

She knew that feeling. She knew it in her bones.

She didn't stop until she couldn't see the bakery any

more, blocked by the gentle curve of the street. The bookshop was barely recognisable, it was a mass of uniformed officers, police vehicles and people in the sort of plastic crime scene suits that Heidi usually only saw on her television screen.

"What's happening here?!"

Heidi spun around, immediately on the defensive, but it was only Kitty.

"There's uh- been an incident," Heidi told her, not sure how much she was allowed to say.

"A break in?!"

Heidi didn't answer, she just chewed her lip uncertainly.

"We haven't had this kind of reaction to any of the thefts so far, what was taken?! Was there damage?!" Kitty pressed.

"No, no theft," Heidi responded, wondering whether that was true.

Had something been stolen? Had Lydia seen someone entering the shop and confronted them? It seemed as though the whole street had been affected by the mystery thief. And now with blackmail added in to the picture? If anyone had secrets to hide, Heidi imagined it would be Lydia Wickes. With the police being totally useless, maybe she had decided to take matters into her own hands.

Watching the bustle and scurry before her, Heidi felt an unexpected pang of sadness at the irony. The police were certainly on the case now.

"What's going on?!" another voice joined the mix, but Heidi kept her eyes fixed on the police moving in and out of Cross-Town Books.

"Something's happened," Kitty replied vaguely, now watching the scene herself.

"What's happened?! Is everyone alright?!"

Heidi turned reluctantly. It was Elizabeth.

"Lydia died," she reported in a small voice. She couldn't keep deflecting people's questions.

"What?!" Kitty and Elizabeth exclaimed in unison.

"How?!"

Heidi didn't answer, once again worrying about how much she should say.

"Miss Cross!"

She flinched as DS Elliot strode towards her, looking exasperated.

"I told you not to leave!" he reminded her hotly.

"I didn't *leave*, I'm right here!" she pointed out.

"That's not what I meant, and you know it."

"How's Rose?" Heidi asked.

"She's with a family liaison officer."

"What happened to Lydia?!" Kitty cut in, making Heidi flinch again.

"You shouldn't be notifying people about the crime!" DS Elliot snapped at Heidi, clearly feeling flustered. Heidi noticed for the first time how young he was. This was probably his first murder case.

"Crime?! You mean she was murdered?!" Kitty gasped.

DS Elliot pressed his finger and thumb to the bridge of his nose for a moment, taking a deep breath.

"I tried not to tell them anything, I thought you might need to make notifications yourself," Heidi told him apologetically.

"Very considerate of you," he muttered drily.

"Was she murdered?!" Kitty demanded, forcing DS Elliot's focus back to her, her voice rising.

"It certainly looks that way," he conceded, mustering his professionalism and carefully smoothing his features into polite sympathy that partially disguised his watchful gaze.

"Oh my gosh! How?! What happened?!"

"She was *stabbed*!" Maggie cried, bursting on the scene as if from nowhere.

"Maggie!" Heidi chastised.

"It's alright dear, Rose is with a nice young woman from the police," Maggie replied comfortably.

"Stabbed?! Where?!" Elizabeth asked.

Maggie and Heidi replied at the same time, their

answers of "In the back" and "In the bookshop" becoming hopelessly entangled.

"What?" Kitty asked, looking from one to the other in bewilderment.

"Lydia. Murdered."

Elizabeth muttered the words quietly, almost to herself but it stopped them all in their tracks. Silence descended and Heidi unexpectedly felt tears prick her eyes.

"Do you think this is connected to the thefts?" Maggie asked Heidi in a whisper when she couldn't bare the quiet any longer.

Heidi just glared at her, but the spell was broken.

"I should go. I need to tell Jane." Elizabeth said suddenly, vanishing across the street.

"I should go too," Kitty announced, casting a last intense look at the bookshop.

DS Elliot watched them both go through narrowed eyes. It wasn't until the three of them were alone that he turned his attention back to them.

"What's all this about thefts?" he asked Maggie.

"I thought that too," Heidi told the older woman, "What if she saw someone letting themselves into the bookshop? What if she confronted them?"

"A good way to get yourself killed!" Maggie agreed, completely ignoring an increasingly frustrated DS Elliot.

"Who let themselves into the bookshop?!" he

demanded.

"Well that's just it, we don't know," Maggie told him.

"If you don't explain what on earth you're talking about, right now, I'm going to arrest you!" he told her, one corner of his mouth twitching against his will.

Maggie set about explaining the circumstance of their unwanted night-time visitor while Heidi relapsed into silence. Something that DS Elliot had said was snagged in her mind.

Who had let themselves in?

Heidi replayed it in her mind. She came downstairs from the flat, she found Lydia, she called the police, retreated out to the street. Had she unlocked the door? She was sure that she hadn't. In fact, the shop keys were probably still on the desk beside the phone base, where she had dropped them so that she could dial emergency services. The shop door had been opened by someone- someone with a key. None of the shops had reported break-ins. The thief had been finding a way in without causing any damage, and now Heidi knew that for the bookshop at least, that method was unlocking the door and then just walking inside. A chill went through her at the thought.

"Who has a key to the shop?" DS Elliot asked suddenly, seeming to read Heidi's thoughts.

"I do, and Maggie and Shelley..." she told him.

"Shelley?"

"She works at the shop part time, around her daughter's school schedule. And..."

"And?"

"Well the thief must have a key. The killer I mean. They must have let themselves in. They've been coming and going this whole time through the front door and I never had any idea."

Chapter 5

After a brief bout of hyperventilating from Maggie, and unnerving disassociation from Heidi, DS Elliot managed to get things back under some semblance of control.

"Sit. Both of you," he instructed, directing them to the seats in the window of the bakery.

Heidi looked around quickly, hoping not to see Rose.

"Rose isn't here," he told her astutely, "the family liaison officer has taken her to her boyfriend's house, to get her away from the crime scene. I understand that the bakery is going to be closed for the rest of the day at least."

"That's good, Robert will look after her," Maggie muttered, settling shakily into a chair.

"Robert? Is that the boyfriend's name?" Elliot asked, making a quick note in his book.

"Yes. Lydia didn't like him," Heidi responded, almost desperately. She didn't want to think that Robert might be a suspect but her mind seemed to be throwing pieces of information at her against her will.

"Why is that?"

"I don't really know. She didn't think he was good enough for Rose. Not successful enough," Heidi offered, wondering if that really had been the reason for Lydia's obvious dislike.

"They can get married now at least," Maggie commented sadly.

"They weren't able to before?" Elliot asked, his tone conversational but his eyes bright with interest.

"Well as we say, Lydia wasn't keen. Rose and her mother are close. It's hard to go against your mother's wishes, isn't it. I'm sure they would have married anyway though!" Maggie finished firmly, squaring her shoulders, ready to defend Rose by whatever means necessary.

"Who else has a key to the bookshop?" the DS asked, turning the conversation.

"We told you, just the three of us and the thief."

Heidi couldn't bring herself to say "killer" this time. The thought was too incomprehensible to be voiced again.

"And how would the thief have gotten a key? If there are only three keys, how would they have one?"

"There are four keys. I have a spare, in my flat. I have two. Maggie has one. Shelley has one."

"Then how could the thief have got ahold of one?" he asked again.

"I have no idea. We reported the thefts, we all did, practically every shop in the street! Nothing was being done about it!" Heidi snapped.

Fear and stress were starting to take a toll and she wished that she could just go home and lock herself away.

"I'm not on that case, or at least I wasn't. If the two do turn out to be connected, then that may change of course," he told her calmly.

"If?! *If* they're connected?! Why else would Lydia have been in the book shop?! Why else would she have been murdered?!" Maggie exclaimed, horrified.

"Can you not think of any other reasons?"

The problem was, Heidi could. She could think of lots of reasons why someone might want Lydia dead. Rose and Robert wanted to get married, Mary wanted the business, everyone found Lydia crushing and cruel. There could be plenty of reasons to murder her, she just couldn't think of any that would end with Lydia lying in the middle of Cross-Town Books.

Heidi's breath seemed to be coming in fives and ones. Not good numbers.

"I want to go home," she muttered involuntarily.

"I'm afraid that wont be possible just yet. The bookshop is being thoroughly searched and we can't risk the crime scene being contaminated further."

"I could go in through the back? There's a door on the next street," she told him.

"We need a little more time."

His tone was sympathetic, but Heidi kept her expression blank. She couldn't think about police searching her beloved bookshop for clues. She didn't want to picture fingerprint powder on the wooden shelves, or crime-scene booties on the colourful, plush rugs.

"What else do you need from us?" Maggie asked.

"I'd like to go over the events of last night and this morning, one more time. Start with this party you mentioned."

One more time turned into two and then three. Shelley joined them after this, her face pale and her hands trembling.

"I was told to come and find you here," she explained to DS Elliot, "is it true? About Lydia?"

This triggered a further recounting of all the events of the morning. Heidi suspected that at this point, she would never forget what happened, no matter how hard she tried.

"This is all just so awful!" Shelley exclaimed, pressing a hand to her mouth as though nauseous.

"Do you have your key to the bookshop with you?" DS Elliot asked her.

"Yes, it's on my key ring with all my others," she told him, obviously confused.

"Can I see it please? All of your keys?"

They dug their keys out of their bags as Heidi

explained that she had left hers in the shop beside the phone.

"That's how I realised that the door had been unlocked. It was still unlocked when I went out that way this morning."

He nodded his comprehension, looking thoughtful.

"I'm going to need to take these with me, I'm afraid. Have any of the keys needed to be replaced? Are any of them new?"

They all shook their heads, Maggie and Shelley unthreading their shop keys from their rings.

"Is there any other reason that Lydia Wickes might have been in the bookshop?" he asked.

"What do you mean?"

"Had she arranged to meet with one of you? One of you three, who has a key?"

They all stared back at him nonplussed.

"You think one of us killed her?" Maggie whispered.

"I didn't say that."

"No, you asked if she met with one of us and ended up dead!"

Although he flushed slightly, DS Elliot remained firm in the face of Maggie's outrage.

"I have no reason to think that any of you killed her, but I do need to ask these questions."

"Where were you and your questions when we were

being stolen from?! Or are the police only in the business of making accusations?!" Maggie demanded.

"I told you, that wasn't my case-" he began, but Heidi cut him off.

"Lydia's ex-husband!"

"Sorry?" Maggie paused mid-tirade and DS Elliot turned to her quickly.

"Lydia's ex-husband! He's some kind of criminal. A scam artist," she explained, waving her hands vaguely.

"Do you know his name?"

"Wouldn't it be Wickes?" Shelley asked.

"Not if she went back to her maiden name," Maggie pointed out.

"What's Rose's last name?" Heidi asked.

"Trent," Maggie supplied.

"So maybe that's the ex-husband's name?"

"I'll find out!" DS Elliot broke in.

All three women descended into disgruntled grumbling. Maggie definitely murmured something about trying to be helpful.

"It's a useful tip, thank you," DS Elliot conceded in some exasperation.

"What are we supposed to do now?" Shelley asked.

Heidi suspected that she already knew the answer. Turning to a fresh page in his notebook, DS Elliot asked them to go over the events just one more time.

"Well that was a waste of a day!" Maggie exclaimed as they finally made their way back across the street.

Heidi could do nothing but sigh. She was so worn down that words just wouldn't come.

"At least they're letting us go home finally," Maggie added, seeing Heidi's pale face.

She nodded, agreeing with this sentiment completely. Shelley had been excused earlier, since she needed to collect her daughter from school and hadn't actually been present when the body was discovered, but Heidi and Maggie had been kept at the bakery for hours. They'd answered every question a dozen times, recounted events more times than that and DS Elliot had watched them closely, seeking out any signs of deception. Heidi had been desperate to leave, but not sure where she would even go. If she couldn't go to her flat, then she had no idea where else she could spend time. The flat, the shop and her running route made up the full extent of her world. Luckily, the crime scene techs gave the all clear just as DS Elliot was checking through the final points in his notebook. The shop was still out of bounds, but she could use the back entrance and take the stairs to her flat, without the risk of compromising anything. Maggie walked her down the street and up the next, not leaving her until they reached the back door.

"Are you sure you're alright? Are you sure you want

to be alone?" she asked anxiously.

"I'm sure. I'm fine," Heidi assured her.

"That DS Elliot," Maggie commented, shaking her head mournfully, "he may be a handsome young thing, but he sure as heck doesn't know how to treat a lady."

"I need a minute." Heidi announced clearly, as she entered her flat, her eyes tightly closed. When she opened them, she let out a slow breath, relieved to find herself alone. She warmed her food and fetched a totally unnecessary blanket before curling up on the sofa and summoning a memory of her mother. It was a little hazy, as so often seemed to be the case now, but it still served its purpose.

"Hey mum," she whispered, as Alice appeared before her.

"Do you want to talk about it, sweetheart?"

"I don't think so. Not yet."

Alice settled in beside her and Heidi did her best to imagine warmth coming from her. It wasn't often that she really longed for physical contact, but this was definitely one of those times. She settled for warm pasta instead, and Funny Face on the the TV, the evening peppered with echoes of her mother's laughter.

As her eyelids started to droop, Heidi surveyed the sofa, wondering whether she should just sleep there. It might be worth it, just to slide into slumber and finally close the book on a horrendous day.

"Keep to your routine!" Joan barked, appearing unbidden in her Queen Anne chair.

"Why? It's not like tomorrow will be a normal day, no matter what I do," Heidi countered.

"That's exactly why you should keep to your routine! Life can throw all sorts of mess at you, you need to be prepared. Make your breakfast now and put it in the fridge. Make your ridiculous coffee drink. Set out your running clothes. Change into real pyjamas and get into a proper bed for a good night's sleep. You need to look after yourself."

There's no one left to do it for you.

Joan didn't say those last words, there was no need. In reality of course, Joan hadn't said anything at all, not for years, it was all Heidi. Heidi talking to herself alone in her flat, imagining all the people that she had lost. Still- that didn't make it bad advice.

With a sigh, she dragged herself up off the sofa and set about preparing for the following day.

She was grateful for her forethought when she woke in the morning, comfortably ensconced in her own bed, with iced coffee waiting in the fridge beside a bowl of chia pudding and fruit. She would start with a run, and then go from there, piecing her day together bit by bit.

"Be careful!"

The words stopped her in her tracks as she was half way out the door. She turned back to find her mother, standing in the middle of the room.

"Be careful! There's a killer out there somewhere!"

It was true of course. Heidi knew that, she had found Lydia on the floor with a knife in her back and had spent the day being questioned by the police, but it somehow hadn't sunk in. Alice spoke the words from the depths of her subconscious, bringing them out into the light of day.

"I will mum," Heidi murmured as she closed the door behind her.

She opened the app on her phone as she started her warm up walk, treading the same route as always, her feet moving unconsciously, following a set pattern that would allow Heidi to focus on what really mattered. The numbers.

She held her phone in her hand the entire time, tracking her pace, her time, her distance and her progress, watching the numbers tick over. She quickened her steps a little, waiting for the average pace to update and drop a second or two. She wanted to get down under twenty five minutes today. That meant keeping each kilometre under five minutes. Five wasn't a very good number, which made it more difficult, but she was running five kilometres and five is the square root of twenty five and so five minutes per kilometre had a nice symmetry to it. Five wasn't a good number, but a chant of five five five, five five five, five five five felt good. She looped the chant around, little clusters of five five five, as she watched the numbers ticking over, tracking her pace minute by minute, number by number until she staggered to a stop, breathing heavily and clutching her side.

Done.

Five kilometres in exactly twenty five minutes. She forced herself to keep walking, keep her legs moving to avoid cramp. She needed to stretch as soon as she got home, her calves were on fire. She rounded the corner and stopped, realising too late that she was going to have to pass the police tape and the chaos that had taken over her shop. If she didn't absolutely hate going back on herself, she would have turned around and walked straight back the way she came. Instead she pushed on, her legs feeling leaden, either from the run or from her reluctance, she couldn't be sure.

In actuality, the shop didn't look too bad. The door was blocked off with police tape, but there were no crime scene technicians today, and no police cars, or white plastic tents reminiscent of CSI. There was a uniformed officer at the door, presumably keeping an eye on things, but that was it. She nodded as Heidi approached, clearly aware of who Heidi was.

"Good run?" she asked brightly, nodding to Heidi's workout gear of leggings and a vest top.

"Yes thanks."

"How far did you go?" the officer asked.

"Just a five-K" Heidi told her, aware of her red face and profusion of sweat.

"*Just*?! I never understand how you runners do it! I gave it a go once, but it's just too hard for me." She sounded perfectly cheerful about the fact but Heidi wondered if really it was something that bothered her.

"It is hard at first. I started small and built up slowly. Now it's much easier," she explained, inwardly cursing herself.

Non-runners never wanted to hear about running. Even runners rarely wanted to hear about it. And 'start small' was the sort of inane advice that could aggravate anybody. The officer only looked to be in her twenties, but she was certainly still old enough to have taken up running if she actually wanted to. In fact, Heidi suspected that a modicum of fitness was required in order to work for the police. She was just starting to wonder whether maybe the woman was lying about running, and the whole conversation might not actually be a trick, when the shop door opened.

"Miss Cross!" DS Elliot exclaimed in surprise.

Maggie was right. He was handsome. Heidi hadn't

noticed it the day before, probably because of all the emotional trauma, but he was actually a very nice looking man. He was tall, with even features, rich brown hair and warm, brown eyes.

"I was running," she blurted unnecessarily.

"So I see," he replied, surveying her sweaty state.

"Not *away*," she clarified.

"Well no, you'd be doing a terrible job of that," he told her with a smile, "coming back here and all."

She flushed even deeper, turning her post workout hue up a notch to a really remarkable vibrancy.

"What are you doing here?" she demanded, trying to claw the situation back under control.

"Investigating a murder, if that's alright."

His tone was light and Heidi suspected that he might actually be laughing at her. She hadn't done anything wrong and couldn't understand why she felt so guilty. She did her best to force the feeling down and stay calm.

"I meant, have you found anything new? In the shop?" she asked.

"Just trying to get a feel for the scene of the crime," he told her.

"Was it? Definitely?"

"Was it definitely what?" he asked, confused.

"Was it definitely the scene of the crime? Did she definitely die here? She wasn't moved here after the fact?"

She had no idea where that question had come from. She wasn't even aware that she had been thinking about it, the words just spilled out.

"Why would you ask that?" DS Elliot asked curiously.

"I don't know. It's just- it's a possibility isn't it?"

He just studied her, his gaze thoughtful. The uniformed officer beside him studied her too, her expression bordering on suspicious.

"When will the shop be able to re-open?" Heidi asked, keen to break in on their scrutiny.

"I'm not sure yet unfortunately. As soon as it can open, I'll let you know. I imagine it must be a busy time of year for you, the summer? And I understand that you have rent to pay."

"No I don't."

"Sorry?"

"I own the shop, and the building it's in, and the flat. I don't have to pay rent. But I would like to get the shop open again as soon as possible," she told him, wishing she'd stayed quiet. She could have just let the comment go, but it wasn't in her nature.

"Gosh, that must be nice!" the officer commented cheerfully, while DS Elliot proceeded to stare at Heidi for another minute of uncomfortable silence.

She forced herself to stay quiet this time, not sure

how to bring the conversation to a close.

"I'm going to go," she stated finally, taking a step away to see whether they would stop her. They didn't, so she quickened her pace, along the road and then down the next, stopping only when she'd shut the door behind her, raced upstairs and was safely shut in her flat once more. Heidi made a mental note to practice some innocuous conversations that she could have with DS Elliot before she saw him next. While she was at it she may as well practice talking to everyone else too. Neighbours and customers alike, were bound to be buzzing about the murder, desperate for details and inside information. Heidi would need to be ready to field their questions. She devised a few simple comments and responses as she showered, letting the water wash away the stress along with the sweat crusting her skin.

Chapter 6

The one good thing about the shop being closed was that it gifted her a day to herself. She stepped out onto the bathmat, wondering what she should read, when her attention was drawn by a knocking on the flat door. This was unusual enough that it caused a shiver to run up Heidi's spine. She rarely got post or deliveries. She *never* had visitors.

"Heidi!" a voice called through the thick oak, as the knocking continued.

"Maggie?"

Heidi twisted her hair up into a towel and pulled on her father's old robe, the red stripes now faded almost to pink.

"The shop is staying closed," Maggie announced as Heidi pulled the door open.

"I know."

"But don't worry dear, I have a plan."

"A plan?" Heidi asked helplessly.

"Yes dear, a plan. I just need your key."

"But we're not allowed into the shop!" Heidi reminded her.

"I won't go into the shop! I'm not a fool! You do have your set of spare keys though, don't you? The police didn't take them?"

Heidi did indeed have her spare set of keys, safely tucked away inside the scroll-top writing desk. Her conscience tugged at her. She knew that she should have offered the keys to DS Elliot but she couldn't bring herself to do it. The thought of having no way to access the bookshop caused an uncomfortable sensation in the pit of her stomach.

"But we're not allowed in the shop!" Heidi repeated.

"I told you! I have no intention of going in there! Don't worry, you just leave everything to me," Maggie assured her, holding out a hand expectantly.

Not sure what else to do, Heidi retrieved the keys and handed them over. Maggie was gone in a swirl of blue tassels and Channel No.5.

Her thoughts trapped in a loop, Heidi returned to the bathroom to brush her hair and continue getting dressed and ready.

Why did Maggie need the keys?

What on earth was she planning?

Heidi asked herself these questions again and again without coming to any kind of satisfactory answer. She had no clue what Maggie was up to and that knowledge made her decidedly uneasy. In the end, she grabbed her iced coffee and headed downstairs to check the door to the shop. True to her word, Maggie hadn't unlocked it, or at least- it was certainly locked now. Heidi exited through the back door and jogged down the street to the end, turning onto Cross Street and heading up it at a brisk trot. She supposed vaguely that she would peer through the front windows of the bookshop and try to detect what Maggie had been up to, but this proved to be unnecessary. When Heidi approached the shopfront, she found Maggie holding court, her plan displayed on a table beside her.

"What's this?"

"Second hand books from the store room!" Maggie told her happily.

It was a clever plan. The store room door was in the back vestibule, opposite the stairs up to the flat. Maggie hadn't had to set a single foot in the shop to get to it. They always had a display of second hand books in the shop, for people without the budget to buy new, or just looking for a bargain. Occasionally in the summer they set up this very table out in front of the shop and had a sale to shift the stock that had mounted too high to be contained. Profits went to charity, since all the books were donated anyway.

"I would have helped set up," Heidi told her, not

sure what else to say.

"That's alright dear, young Robert helped me. Besides, you were only just out of the shower and I wanted to be up and running as quickly as possible so that I don't miss a single thing!"

"What do you mean? Miss what?"

"The show!" Maggie gestured to the street before them as she spoke, like a ringmaster introducing the next incredible act in a circus.

Following her gaze, Heidi saw what she meant. Uniformed officers were entering Luscious Whisper. Jane and Elizabeth were both hovering on their front step, talking quietly amongst themselves and Kitty watched with narrowed eyes from outside her own shop. Even Mr Price and Mr Bingley stood together, watching the proceedings and muttering darkly. When they spotted the book stall they both hurried over, their eyes bright with interest.

"Tell us *everything*!"

"Where would you like me to start?" Maggie asked with relish.

"At the beginning, dear lady!" Mr Price replied with a theatrical bow.

"Is it true that it was Lydia Wickes? The woman who hosted the party?" Mr Bingley interjected.

"Oh yes! Stabbed! Heidi came downstairs yesterday morning and found her on the floor, dead!"

All eyes turned to Heidi, who stood rooted to the floor.

"That must have been awful for you!" Bingley exclaimed sympathetically.

"Such a tragedy," Heidi murmured in agreement, pleased to be able to use one of her practised comments.

"Do the police know what happened?" Mr Price asked, leaning forward eagerly, his eyes roving from Maggie to Heidi and back again.

"They didn't seem to know anything at all yesterday, but I haven't seen them since then," Maggie reported.

"They didn't really say much to me this morning," Heidi added.

"You saw them this morning?!" Maggie asked quickly, turning to Heidi with interest.

"DS Elliot and another officer were here, looking around the shop again."

Heidi considered voicing the suggestion that she had made to DS Elliot, that Lydia might have been murdered elsewhere, but she decided against it. She didn't want to get caught up in the speculation. Besides, who was she to be devising theories?

"Who would want to murder Lydia?" Mr Bingley wondered aloud.

They all looked at him uncertainly, no one prepared to answer the question.

"I haven't been here long, I know, but I did pick up on certain... tensions," he added.

"Lydia wasn't an easy person to get along with," Mr Price suggested tactfully.

"Because she was awful. Cruel, insensitive and mean," Maggie added far less tactfully.

"Not quite a reason to murder someone, surely?!" Mr Bingley reproached.

"I suppose that would depend on who she was cruel, insensitive and mean to," Maggie replied.

"But do you really think that's why she was killed?" Heidi blurted out.

"What do *you* suggest?" Mr Price asked her.

"Well, I assumed that she was killed by whoever has been breaking in to the shops in the street. If she saw someone breaking into the bookshop, she might have confronted them and been murdered because of it."

Mr Price and Mr Bingley both looked thoughtful.

"A solid theory," Mr Price commented with obvious approval.

"Someone mentioned the thefts and break-ins. I haven't had anything like that happen at my place, thank goodness. Do you really think the thief could be a killer?" Mr Bingley asked them all.

"A thief and a blackmailer! Who knows what someone like that could be capable of?!" Maggie responded with a shudder.

"Mr Price," Heidi began suddenly, "You've had thefts at your shop too, haven't you?"

"I have indeed. Though no blackmail, thank goodness. I lead far too dull a life for that."

"Was a window broken? Or the lock forced? Do you know how they got in?" Heidi asked him.

"The police officer that I spoke to suggested that I had left the door unlocked by mistake. He also pointed out a small window at the back that the thief could have used if they were a circus acrobat."

Mr Price was clearly unimpressed by these suggestions.

"Tsk! We were told the same thing! We must have forgotten to lock the door- we should be glad the lock hadn't been damaged- we're lucky a window wasn't smashed. It's shoddy police work!" Maggie told him bitterly.

"But they have a key! The door was definitely locked the night before the murder, and definitely *unlocked* when I found Lydia's body. Somehow, the thief got a key to Cross-Town Books! I'm going to get our locks changed as soon as the police are done with the shop. You should get your locks changed too!" Heidi told Mr Price.

"A key?! But how-" he broke off suddenly, his expression thoughtful.

"A few months ago, I thought I had lost my keys. I turned the whole shop upside down, I looked everywhere. It turned out I had dropped them in the street outside. Kitty found them and returned them to me. They were all there, so I didn't think any more about it!"

They all let this sink in. Heidi's gaze was drawn across the street to where Kitty watched Luscious Whisper through narrowed eyes. For the first time, Heidi really acknowledged to herself that she believed someone in the street had been breaking into other shops. That meant that someone in the street was a killer.

Chapter 7

Heidi took refuge in her flat for lunch, leaving Maggie to man the book stall in the street alone.

"What on earth is that woman up to?!" Joan demanded, "can't she go two minutes without gossip?!"

"Are you alright Heidi, my love?" Alice asked gently.

"I think it's brilliant!"

At these words, Joan and Alice dimmed. Heidi hadn't seen her father since they'd discovered the loss of the bell, too anxious to imagine what he would say.

"Brilliant?" Heidi asked a little breathlessly.

"Absolutely! Get a wriggle on Nancy Drew! You've got a killer to catch!"

"What do you mean?! I run a bookshop!" Heidi protested.

"A book shop full of crime books! Thrillers! Mysteries! You'd read every novel Agatha Christie ever published by the time you were twelve! I'm sure you can solve one measly murder!"

He beamed and Heidi felt her own lips twitch in

response. She longed to reach out to him, to feel the scratchiness of his jumper, the prickle of his stubble when she kissed his cheek. She could almost smell the scent of soap and toast and old paper, that was the very essence of her father.

"Dad, you're mad," she told him affectionately, something that she and her mother used to tell him all the time.

"All the best people are!"

Heidi paced the kitchen between chopping vegetables and mixing dressing. She walked to the fridge and then the counter and then back to the fridge in a daze.

Solve a murder?!

There was no way she could do that! She wasn't qualified! Except that- well- she did know the people in the street better than the police did. She'd been watching her neighbours from a distance for years now, seeing their stories play out day by day. She knew Lydia too. She'd watched her tear people down and cut them to the quick with her 'innocent remarks'. Her dad was right too, she knew every Agatha Christie. Every Patricia Wentworth and Margery Allingham too for that matter. She'd consumed more mystery novels than she'd had actual social interactions.

I could solve a murder!

Heidi practically wolfed down her finally assembled salad before topping up her iced coffee from the cafetière in the fridge and marching back downstairs into battle. Maggie was still manning the stall, but Shelley had joined her and the two were working their way through pasta salads while chatting with Elizabeth between bites.

"Hello Elizabeth," Heidi greeted her as she joined them.

Instead of the greeting that she was expecting, Elizabeth offered only the smallest of nods and then hurried away, back across the street towards the dress shop.

"What was that?" Heidi asked the other two.

"Oh dear."

"What?" she demanded.

Maggie and Shelley both squirmed uncomfortably.

"Well dear, it seems that some people are a little bit nervous of you," Maggie admitted.

"Nervous of me?! Why?"

This reversal of roles was unexpected and definitely wouldn't help Heidi with her investigation.

"Well, because Lydia's body was found in the bookshop." Shelley supplied.

"What so- they think *I* killed her?!"

"No no! Of course not!" Maggie exclaimed, "at least, no one has said that to *me*... but they do seem to think that you might be cursed."

"Cursed?" Heidi muttered to herself.

Unfortunately it made sense. Losing her parents so young, losing Joan, then a body turning up practically at her feet. It was bound to make people uncomfortable. That much proximity to death was surely unusual for someone her age.

"It's just because you and Joan lived so quietly. And you've carried on living quietly ever since. People are always a little bit afraid of what they don't know, and they haven't had the opportunity to know you," Maggie told her reasonably.

"You are a bit of a mystery," Shelley added, almost apologetically.

Heidi inwardly cringed at this. She'd tried to keep herself to herself, just like Joan had taught her, but instead she'd managed to make herself into a spectacle.

"I never meant to be a *mystery*," she told them desperately.

"I know dear, but beautiful young women aren't supposed to live like elderly spinsters! It makes you seem a bit of a conundrum."

"You just need to put yourself out there more!" Shelley told her brightly.

"I'm going to," Heidi announced with decision.

"You are?"

"Yes. I am. I'm going to solve Lydia's murder."

"Well I'm sure that'll make you seem much more normal," Maggie commented placidly.

"That's not really what I meant," Shelley told her in a small, forlorn voice.

"I'm going to figure out who killed Lydia, and get justice," Heidi repeated, enjoying the way the words sounded aloud, even if they were a tad theatrical.

"I meant something like speed dating," Shelly murmured.

"Do you have a plan?" Maggie enquired with interest.

"To find out who killed Lydia."

"Excellent. Good to know you have all the details figured out."

"Well I'll talk to people. I'll find out who might have wanted to kill Lydia. Means, motive and opportunity. Who had access? Who wanted her dead? Who had a great big knife?" Heidi rambled, trying to get her thoughts in line.

"Lots of people wanted to kill Lydia though. She was horrible," Shelley pointed out.

"Yes. But like Mr Bingley pointed out, most of the time people don't get murdered for being horrible," Heidi countered.

"So why *do* people get murdered?"

An excellent question. Why do people kill? Heidi mentally ran through the catalogue of crimes she'd read about.

"Money. Money is a big motivator for murder. And Jealousy and love and everything, but money seems to come up a lot," she said thoughtfully.

"You're thinking of the thief?" Maggie asked.

"Actually I wasn't. That's definitely still a possibility-if someone has been stealing and blackmailing in the street and Lydia caught them, they might have killed her just to keep from getting in trouble. But I was actually thinking about other people who might get money from Lydia dying. Mary for one."

"Mary?! But she's so quiet!" Shelley objected.

"It's always the quiet ones!" Maggie announced cheerfully.

"But she wanted the business. And you heard her, she thought she would get it all to herself once Lydia was gone. I wonder if that's true..." Heidi trailed off thoughtfully, wondering how exactly one goes about discovering the contents of a will.

"It doesn't really matter if it's true or not, does it? It just matters that Mary believed it," Maggie pointed out, her expression suddenly grim.

"You don't really think it was Mary, do you?!" Shelley asked.

"It was someone," Maggie told her, her mouth a thin line and her brows furrowed.

"Would you rather it was Rose?" Heidi asked, making Shelley gasp.

"Of course not! It couldn't be Rose! Not her own daughter!"

"But that's exactly the point. Lydia was her mother- she might stand to inherit now Lydia's dead. She might get money, or even the business. And she can marry Robert now too, Lydia wont be able to stand in their way any more."

Maggie looked deeply saddened by this suggestion but Shelley was just shaking her head in absolute denial.

"It couldn't be Rose! She's so nice!" she insisted.

"Some killers are charming," Heidi told her, dredging up her recollections of the true-crime books she'd read. She was definitely more of a fiction person, but she could never turn down a good read.

"Ted Bundy charmed most of his victims. And John Wayne Gacy, and countless others! They seemed like such nice people that no one could believe they were capable of killing."

Shelley and Maggie were both quiet, pondering her words. Heidi noted that whereas Shelley looked distressed at the very suggestion, Maggie's expression leant more toward speculative.

"We have to consider Robert too then," she declared, making Heidi's lips twitch.

"That's a good point! He could just have wanted Lydia out of the way so that he cold marry Rose, or he could even have been the thief! He could have been stealing to have more money to impress Lydia! Trying to win her over so that he could marry Rose with her blessing!"

"But Lydia's shop was stolen from too, wasn't it? That would be too risky!" Shelley exclaimed.

"Yes, Lydia said money was stolen. But if he thought he'd never be caught..."
Heidi could see that Shelley still wanted to argue the point, so she cut in quickly.

"Rose and Robert definitely make the list, and Mary too. And there's the mystery thief. Did anyone else benefit from Lydia's death?"

"What are you three talking about?"

They all spun round, faces flushed and eyes wide, to find Kitty with her arms crossed and eyes narrowed in obvious judgement.

"Just- um... talking about Lydia," Shelley stammered uncomfortably.

"So I heard."

"Don't be to sanctimonious Kitty! You detested Lydia!" Maggie scolded, rearranging the folds of her shawl as though completely unconcerned.

"I did not *detest* her!" Kitty whispered, casting an

anxious look at the police presence across the road.

"Oh, best of friends were you?" Maggie retorted, "we all saw that scene the other day, and we were all at the party."

Kitty paled.

"That doesn't mean I killed her!" she hissed.

"And who on earth said you did?!" Maggie demanded in exasperation.

"Are you really being blackmailed?" Heidi asked abruptly.

"What?!"

Kitty looked almost frantic now.

"Who told you that?! What are people saying?! None of this has anything to do with- well- with anything!"

And just like that she spun one hundred and eighty degrees and marched away, back down the street.

"That wasn't very delicate," Maggie critiqued.

"No, but it did confirm that she's being blackmailed," Heidi replied thoughtfully.

"She didn't want anyone to talk about her argument with Lydia either, did she," Shelley commented.

"Very true! She seemed very upset by the idea of the police finding out about it!" Maggie agreed.

"No! Now you've got me doing it too!" Shelley cried, "Kitty didn't kill anyone! She's a perfectly nice person!"

Shelley crossed her arms and refused to be drawn any

further into speculation. While Heidi and Maggie discussed suspects and theories, she remained stony silent, not saying a word until another figure appeared on the scene.

"Rose!"

Shelley stood up and held her arms out, but Rose bypassed her entirely, side stepping Maggie and flinging her arms around Heidi who was completely unprepared for so much affection.

Don't flinch. Don't flinch. Don't flinch.

She repeated the words in her head as she patted Rose on the back, in what she hoped was a soothing manner.

"The police said you found her!" Rose said, finally stepping back and gazing intently into Heidi's face.

"Yes, yes I did," Heidi agreed uselessly.

"They wont tell me anything! Was it awful?! Did it look like she was hurt?" Rose fired off, fumbling to clasp hold of Heidi's hands.

Make eye contact. It's alright not to smile.

"What have the police said?" Heidi asked, not sure where to start.

"They said they suspect murder, but no more than that! Murder! I can't believe it, it just sounds crazy!"

Heidi took a breath, buying herself time. There was no way that Rose wouldn't hear the details, now that they were circulating in the street. She wished the police had filled her in, but they clearly didn't understand how the rumour mill worked in their little community.

"When I came downstairs yesterday morning, I found her in the bookshop," she explained tentatively, "and she'd obviously been stabbed. There was a knife."

Heidi let these words sink in. She could practically see it happen. The truth settled into Rose's eyes and then slipped beneath the surface, into the depths.

"Someone stabbed her?" she asked in a small voice.

"Yes."

"There was a knife? You actually saw a knife?" she asked.

"Yes."

Heidi decided against mentioning that the knife was still embedded in Lydia's back. It seemed the sort of thing that might be deemed insensitive.

"A knife from the bookshop?" Rose asked in a daze, her knees starting to tremble, causing her to waver where she stood.

"Here darling, sit down!" Maggie exclaimed, drawing her chair up behind Rose and gently easing her back into it.

"I was sure it was going to turn out to be some kind of mistake... an accident or something, you know?" she murmured, looking up at them hopelessly, "but... stabbed."

Shelley and Maggie cooed over her, holding her hands and stroking her hair, but Heidi just stood, her mind snagged on something Rose had said.

The knife wasn't from the shop. The bookshop, fairly obviously, didn't *have* knives. So where had it come from? If Lydia had witnessed someone entering the shop to steal, and had come to confront that person, would she have come armed? Would she really bring a knife into the mix? Perhaps if she too was being blackmailed. Or perhaps she had seen someone that she already knew was dangerous.

"Rose have you contacted your father?" Heidi blurted, drawing three pairs of eyes.

"My dad?" Rose asked blankly.

"Yes. I mean- does he know about your mum? Is he coming to- to look after you?" Heidi asked, trying to smooth out any awkwardness but not prepared to let go of her point.

"I don't even know where he is," Rose choked, her eyes suddenly filling with fresh tears.

"You don't know where he is?" Heidi repeated.

"I haven't even heard from him in a few years now. I have no idea where he is! He hasn't been around in forever, and he was never exactly dependable but-" she cut off, a sob overwhelming her as she buried her face in her hands.

"You have Robert, anyway," Shelley reminded her

comfortingly.

"Yes, Robert." Rose muttered in an incredibly small voice.

"Things are alright with you and Robert aren't they?! He's taking good care of you?" Maggie asked quickly, giving Heidi the briefest of winks.

"Yes- I- yes of course. Robert loves me."

"Still, this must have been a huge shock and that can be a strain on a relationship," Maggie suggested thoughtfully.

Rose chewed on her lip, not looking at any of them.

"No! Robert's lovely! He and Rose are so happy!" Shelley cut in defiantly.

Strangely it was this that goaded Rose to speech. Colour crept into her cheeks and her expression was plaintive.

"I know that Robert loves me but- but mum hated him! She was awful to him! And now- now she's-"

she stuttered to a halt, looking stricken.

"Are you just hurt that he's not grieving like you are, or are you actually worried he might have been involved?" Heidi asked.

She knew immediately that it was the wrong thing to say. Maggie and Shelley both flinched slightly and Rose burst up from her seat, with fire in her eyes.

"Robert would never hurt *anyone*! He's wonderful!

And he loves me! He'd never hurt my mum!" she shouted, stepping in so close to Heidi that it made her wince.

"I'm sorry," Heidi told her but couldn't go on.

"Don't you say *anything* about Robert!" Rose finished, storming off at full speed.

Heidi stayed, frozen in place, as she slowed her breathing. Confrontation wasn't something that she had much experience of but it definitely wasn't something that she enjoyed.

"Perhaps that wasn't the most tactful you've ever been dear," Maggie commented gently.

"But she wasn't clear! She could have meant either!" Heidi argued helplessly.

"She probably meant both," Maggie replied sadly.

"Both?! Then what was I supposed to say?! How are you supposed to respond when someone is saying two things at once?!"

Neither woman had an answer for this so Heidi had to be satisfied with collapsing back into her seat and taking a large sip of her iced coffee.

"Do you think I should get some cakes?" Shelley asked when the mood hadn't improved in another quarter of an hour.

"I think cake sounds like an excellent idea!" Maggie agreed with a relieved sigh.

Shelley hurried off to secure sugary sustenance while

Heidi and Maggie remained, slumped in their seats, feeling dejected.

"It's actually quite unpleasant trying to think of everyone as a murder suspect, isn't it," Maggie commented forlornly.

"It's definitely easier in books."

"At least Rose didn't seem guilty!" Maggie said, suddenly brightening.

"True. She seemed more worried about us suspecting Robert."

"And that wouldn't be the case if she was the killer, would it?!"

Maggie was so obviously cheered by this thought that Heidi couldn't bring herself to correct her. She wasn't going to point out that sometimes killers lie and pretend, to cover up their crimes.

"Cakes!" Shelley announced, rejoining them and flopping into her seat with a huff.

"You look worn out! What happened?!" Maggie asked.

"Nothing! Nothing!"

"*Shelley*,"

"It's nothing really, just- Zoe who works at the bakery with Rose, made a comment or two," she told them vaguely.

"A comment or two? What's that supposed to

mean?" Maggie demanded, heedless of Shelley's pleading look.

"Apparently she's heard about the supposed curse and she didn't want to sell me the cakes. I had to make a bit of a fuss actually," Shelley admitted, blushing furiously and refusing to meet Heidi's eye.

"What, she thinks if she sells me a cake, she's going to drop dead?!"

"Something like that. She's probably just being difficult so that she can feel all involved and important," Shelley said consolingly.

Heidi looked down at her cream slice, suddenly not sure whether she wanted it. It felt tainted.

"You eat that cream slice Heidi!" Maggie cried, "it's the spoils of war! That silly woman wanted to keep you from having it, but Shelley went to bat and now a cream slice you have!"

Through the jumble of metaphors, the meaning hit home. Heidi smiled and took a large bite, carefully prodding the overly-enthusiastic cream back into place with her little finger.

"Thank you," she said to Shelley, earning herself a warm smile in return.

"Can you believe this?!"

All three women looked up from their cakes, with the expressions of guilty school children, expecting to be confronted with the calorie police. Instead they saw Mary, striding across the street towards them from the direction of Luscious Whisper.

"Mary!" Maggie called in greeting, making quick work of the last of her cream slice and then bouncing to her feet.

"We were all so sorry to hear about Lydia."

These words brought Mary up short. She froze, one foot in the air, mid step.

"What? Oh! Oh yes, of course!"

"You worked for her for so long, this must have been a terrible shock," Maggie suggested in her most comforting manner.

"Well yes, it is a shock of course. No one sees something like this coming. But really, I think the best thing for me would be to get on with work! But the police wont allow it!"

She'd circled round to her real grievance and was obviously determined to have her say.

"They won't let me in! I can't take the books or the computer or anything! They wouldn't even let me *touch* anything!"

"But why do you want them? The computer and things I mean," Shelley asked in bewilderment.

"I need to be getting on with things! Like I said, I need to be busy! I need to get back to work but they won't let me! They wont give me any idea of when the shop can open either, which is crazy because Lydia wasn't even killed there!"

She was practically shrieking now, her voice shrill with hysteria.

"Someone was murdered, they need to investigate. They'll need to look into the business and look for motive. I imagine they're searching the shop to look for any reason someone might have wanted Lydia dead," Heidi explained slowly.

"But it's *my* shop! It's *mine* now! It has nothing to do with Lydia! And she wasn't even killed there! Besides, what do they think they're going to find?! The shop was doing fine! Great even! We had plenty of money coming in!"

They all just stood, watching uncomfortably as Mary wrung her hands and gazed anxiously across the street. She seemed to sense that her words weren't going down particularly well, and spun back around, her expression imploring.

"I just want to find my footing, you know? The business is mine now and I want to start getting to grips with things! Lydia wouldn't want the business to fall apart! That's understandable, isn't it?" she demanded.

It was. Heidi could understand it perfectly, but she could also see why the police wouldn't. Heidi had opened the shop as usual the day after her aunt Joan had died.

She'd gone over every detail of the running of the business. She already knew it all, she'd been learning it since she was eight years old, but she wanted to be absolutely sure that she could carry on on her own. The only way to be sure, was to sift through the details and then start. To her, it made sense for Mary to want to get started as soon as possible, but there was a frenzy to her manner that was a little unsettling. It made Heidi wonder whether there might not be more to this. Was there something on the computer that Mary didn't want the police to see? Something in the businesses books that she wanted to hide?

"It's good the shop's been doing so well. You weren't hit too hard by the thefts on the street?" Heidi asked, wondering how to find out more about the shop's finances.

"We had a couple of thefts. Some stock was stolen, but luckily insurance covered it. And some money was taken, but that was actually mine," Mary admitted, running a hand through her hair distractedly.

"Yours?"

"Yes. Mine. I left my bag in the shop overnight by mistake and that was the night we were broken in to."

"Broken in to? Was it a window? Or door?" Heidi asked with interest.

"Oh, I just meant 'broken in' as a figure of speech. I actually have no idea how they got in. Everything looked secure the next morning, but the police think I must have just forgotten to lock up. There's a window at the back, but it's pretty small and I don't often leave it open anyway! Lydia was furious with me! She went on and on about-" she cut off, flushing guiltily.

"It's alright," Maggie told her consolingly, "we all know how Lydia treated you."

Mary cast a wary look back across the street at the police officers flitting in and out of Luscious Whisper and gave a small shrug.

"It wasn't so bad," she offered feebly.

"She made you *work* the party the other night!" Shelley reminded her.

"I didn't mind that- I was an employee. The whole reason Lydia agreed to leave me the shop was because she knew I was prepared to go above and beyond," she countered defensively.

"Then why didn't she make you a partner years ago?" Maggie asked shortly.

"Well she built the business herself and... she liked to have things a certain way but- she always respected me. She just wasn't very good at showing it, but she wouldn't have agreed to leave me the business if she didn't respect me!"

Mary sounded almost desperate now. Her words turned Heidi's stomach over. She felt a sharp pang of pain at Mary's obvious heartbreak.

"Everyone expresses themselves differently," Maggie offered, reaching out one hand and patting Mary's shoulder gently. It was a small gesture and no one thought she really meant it, but her sympathy was obviously sincere and Mary forced a small smile.

"I should go. If they're not going to let me into the shop, I should go home and try to find something else to get on with," she told them, dabbing at her eyes and giving a brave sigh before walking away.

"Poor Mary," Shelley commented sadly.

"Yes," Maggie replied thoughtfully, her tone lacking any real agreement.

"Did you notice her eyes?" Heidi asked.

"I did."

"Her eyes?" Shelley asked.

"She dabbed at them before she left, but she wasn't actually crying. She seems more upset about the business than about Lydia," Heidi explained.

"Well that's because Lydia was horrible to her!" Shelley argued.

"Exactly."

"No! Mary wouldn't do this! She wouldn't kill Lydia to get the business or for any other reason!" Shelley exclaimed.

Heidi wasn't so sure. She couldn't help feeling that of all the suspects on the list, Mary should likely be at the very top. She even had a nagging suspicion that Mary had said something important that she, Heidi, had missed.

It wasn't until she was climbing into bed that night that she worked it out. It was her dad who made the suggestion of course- the man who had read her every single Nancy Drew mystery.

"Why would someone move a body?" he asked, perched on the side of the bed, right where he used to sit when she was little.

"We don't know that anybody *did* move the body," she pointed out.

"But we don't know that they didn't. Which means-"

"That we should at least consider the possibility," she finished.

"Exactly! So I ask again, why would someone move a body?"

"Because they didn't want the crime to be tied to them. If the body is found in their own living room, its pretty clear that they're the killer," Heidi suggested.

"Right, that's one possibility. If the body was found in the bakery, the police would go straight to Rose," her father agreed.

"But I don't think Rose did it."

"You don't know for sure though, so you can't rule her out! What other reasons- why else might someone move a body?" he pressed.

"For convenience," she answered slowly.

"Give your reasoning-" he prompted, like he was helping her to think through a homework assignment.

"Mary. Mary wants the shop open. She wants access to everything inside the business. If the body was found in Luscious Whisper, then the police would be sure to close the shop and she would be shut out."

"But that happened anyway," her dad pointed out reasonably.

"Yes- but Mary was really surprised. She couldn't understand why the police were searching the shop! She outright said that she couldn't understand it since the crime hadn't been committed there!" Heidi finished in excitement.

"That shop could be a crime scene!" her dad agreed happily.

They were both practically bouncing up and down now, but Heidi tried to calm herself.
"The police have been in Luscious Whisper all day, if it was a crime scene, surely they would have noticed."

"But they weren't looking for that were they? They were looking for motive! They *should* have been looking for blood!"

Phillip Cross beamed at his daughter ecstatically. It was time for her to break out of her comfort zone, and into a neighbouring premises.

"Tell me again why you're not just calling the police?" Joan demanded as Heidi pulled on some exercise gear. She'd decided that leggings and a t-shirt was more burglar/crime-fighter appropriate than pyjamas.

"And say what? I think you might have missed a huge chunk of evidence at Lydia's shop?" Heidi queried.

"Yes!"

"They'd have no reason to listen to me! They might even think I'm the killer trying to de-rail their investigation! Or just trying to get involved like some psycho who's committed a crime!" Heidi countered.

"So let me get this straight. To avoid looking guilty, you're going to commit an actual crime, by breaking into what might be a real-live crime scene?" Joan demanded.

"That's a really good point!" her dad chimed in, "You'll need gloves!"

Heidi didn't much like gloves, so she only owned mittens herself, but after a bit of digging she found an old pair that had belonged to Joan.

"You can't wear those! Don't you dare bring *me* into this!" Joan complained.

"Perfect!" Phillip exclaimed, clapping his hands together at the sight of the full ensemble.

"Maybe this is a bad idea," Heidi suggested, suddenly seized by doubts at the last moment.

"Thank you!" Joan cried triumphantly.

"This is a *murder investigation*! A little risk is *necessary*! You could at least go over there and see if there's a way in. If there isn't, well then no harm, no foul," Phillip suggested.

Joan fumed, but didn't say a word. Her father had won the argument and they all knew it.

"I'll be back soon!" Heidi whispered, slipping out the door. She just made out the sound of her mother's voice, asking her to be careful, before it clicked shut.

The street wasn't nearly as dark as she would have liked. Heidi wondered whether she should go home and wait until later, once the street lights were out and she could make her way fully cloaked in darkness. If she didn't think that she would likely lose her nerve entirely, she would have turned back then. Instead, she walked quickly across the street, trying to look nonchalant. She knew that she presented an odd spectacle in her black leggings and black t-shirt, especially with Joan's red woollen winter gloves, but she hoped that if she acted naturally, no one would be alarmed. The trouble was, it's actually very hard to act naturally on purpose. As soon as she formed the intention, Heidi completely forgot what she was supposed to do with her arms. Did they swing at her side? In time with her steps, or not? Maybe she was swinging them too much- but she didn't want to look stiff either. Even just putting one foot in front of another like a normal human being was suddenly too much. She practically ran the last few steps to the door, just to get the short journey over with.

It was locked.

She wasn't sure exactly what she'd been expecting- the police were unlikely to leave the place unsecured- but it was still a disappointment. She half-heartedly checked the windows, though she knew that they didn't open, and she'd almost given up entirely when she remembered something else that Mary had said- there was a window around the back that occasionally stayed open. She'd said that it was small, but so was Heidi!

She jogged quickly to the next street, looking for the access to the back of Luscious Whisper. After walking back and forth over one stretch of the street, she spotted a small sign for the trade entrance. Trust Lydia not to allow deliveries to the front of the building. Instead there was a back door, also locked, and a window that stood slightly ajar. Mary was right, it *was* small. Even Heidi would struggle to fit, though she thought that she could probably make it if she could get up high enough. The window was a good five foot off the ground, and Heidi had to push up onto her tip-toes just to see through it to the darkness of the shop. She wasn't able to make out much of anything, but couldn't see any movement inside. If she could get in, she should be able to have a good look around without being discovered. She cast her gaze about her, looking for something to climb on to. Two doors down there was an industrial bin, pulled out ready for collection. She strolled over to it, utterly casual, and leant against it, trying to look like she was just resting, propped up against a bin, something that anybody might do. She tested the weight and found that with some effort, she was able to roll the bin along on it's wheels, jolting and bumping on the cobble stones. When she had it positioned underneath the window she stepped back. Was there any way to climb onto the bin subtly, and get through the window in a way that would look natural and un-suspicious?

Probably not.

The best she could do was stay as quiet as possible and try not to fall off. Getting onto the bin proved to be almost as hard as climbing through the window would have been, but eventually she was up, crouched on top of the convex lid, feeling it sag worryingly beneath her. Heidi wasn't sure what the bin contained but she was fairly sure that she didn't want to collapse into it. Whatever she was going to do, she should probably do it quickly. She lifted the window, testing gingerly to make sure that it didn't catch part-way open like a lot of safety windows. She was in luck- the window swung wide in her grip and she was able to stick her head in and look around. There was nothing under the window, just a straight drop down to the floor at the back of the shop. Heidi pulled her head back and shuffled around, keeping her balance through sheer willpower. When she'd completed a full one hundred and eighty degree rotation, she reached to lever the window open with one hand before sliding her feet in. She silently congratulated herself for wearing leggings, as she slid slowly backward, the window kept open by her body, sliding up her legs as she slid through. It was a tight squeeze at her hips, and then the weight of her legs dangling down caused a definite shift in her centre of gravity. Suddenly she was sliding much quicker off of the curved bin lid, and towards the floor, as her fingers scrambled for a hold. She scraped one shoulder through her t-shirt as she finally dropped to the floor, in more of a tangled heap than she would have liked. She jumped up, dusting herself off, and looking around instinctively to make sure she hadn't been seen. There was no way that she could get back out of that window, but she would have to find another way once she'd uncovered what she came for.

The shop was completely dark. Heidi switched on the torch on her phone, covering it with her hand to block the glow. Carefully, she pointed it towards the back wall, away from the exposure of the large front windows, and removed her hand. Shelves of products and racks of skimpy garments met her eye. As the beam travelled she saw more and more items, some of which she didn't even recognise. Heidi's understanding of romance came straight out of a Jane Austen novel, and she couldn't imagine the characters of Sense and Sensibility perusing a shop like this.

She kept walking, slowly making her way along the back wall of the shop, wondering where someone would commit a murder. Would Lydia have been restocking the shelves? Unlikely in the middle of the night. Perhaps she would have been at the till? But no- the desk had been turned into the bar for the party. Heidi needed to think about this logically. It would help if she knew what time Lydia had died. Had she been home after the party, and then come back to the shop for some reason? Had she only been killed minutes before Heidi found her? In which case she could have been murdered shortly after arriving for work early. Or maybe she'd been killed not long after the party finished, whatever time that was.

Heidi stopped, closing her eyes and slowing her breathing. In for three, out for four. She tried to picture the scene- she'd walked down the stairs, pushed open the door, and seen Lydia lying on the floor.

What had she been wearing? She remembered a black coat. Not a thick, winter one, just a light summer trench coat, but still- a coat. Then there had been bare legs and a pair of ridiculously high heels. She must have been coming straight from the party. It made sense- if she had stayed at the shop to put everything to rights and get it ready for the next day, she would have been one of the only people awake in the whole street, in the middle of the night. Just Lydia, alone in the shop, perhaps with Mary there to help her.

Then there was her arm. Heidi had reached out and touched it, she'd looked for a pulse. Lydia had already felt cold. She'd been dead for some time.

So that meant that Lydia could have been killed anywhere in Luscious Whisper. If she was tidying up, she could have been standing anywhere at all when someone crept up behind her with a knife. It didn't even have to be Mary, Heidi realised. Lydia might have left the door unlocked while she cleaned and straightened up. Mary could have been long gone and Lydia could have been alone and vulnerable, all by herself in the shop in the middle of the night. Just like Heidi was now.

A sudden sound cut through the dark.

On instinct, Heidi dropped down to a crouch and crab shuffled to the closest shelves, desperately hoping that they would block her from view. She cast a hopeless look at the window, wishing she'd found some other point of egress. She heard what sounded like a key being fitted into a lock, followed by the 'tap tap' of shoes on the hard floor, moving further and further into the shop.

Who could it be?! The killer returned to the scene of

the crime?! At least she would find out who it was, before they murdered her too.

"Hello?" a voice called.

It was a voice that she recognised, even if it wasn't entirely familiar. She scrabbled to place it but her heart was pounding in her ears and making it hard to think. Do murderers call out to their victims before they kill them? Possibly to lure them out into the open...

"Hello?" the call came again.

She tried to make herself as small as possible, folding in on herself, painfully aware that her exercise gear would be no protection at all from a knife. She started scanning the closest racks and shelves, looking for anything that could be used as a weapon, but she didn't think that a pair of frilly knickers was going to do her any good here, and there was nothing else in reach. She had walked in here entirely unprepared and now she was going to pay for it with her life.

"Hello? This is DS Elliot. I'm going to need you to step out, with your hands on show."

Wait. What?!

"Please step out, keeping your hands in view," he called, still in the middle of the shop.

Heidi tried to think out a plan of action, an excuse for her being there, anything at all! Unfortunately she was just too relieved that DS Elliot wasn't a crazed killer to come up with much of anything. She slowly unfolded to standing, putting her hands up above her head like she'd seen in movies, and shuffled out into view.

"Hello!" she called feebly, "it's only me!"

"Miss Cross?!"

"Yes, I'm- I'm sorry," she called.

DS Elliot looked confused and suspicious, but her manner clearly wasn't that of a master criminal, so he seemed to be swinging in the direction of annoyance.

"What are you doing here?!" he demanded.

"Should I not be here? There wasn't any crime-scene tape on the door. And no sign or anything."

"That's not the point! You shouldn't- look- just answer the question! Why are you here?" he snapped.

"I was looking for something."

"Looking for what?! In the middle of the night?! It must be something very important."

Heidi said nothing. She should have prepared a cover story in advance, but she hadn't intended to be caught!

"Alright, look. Do you have any weapons on you?" he asked when she didn't say anything.

Heidi eyed the rack of ruffled pink panties to her left.

"No."

"Good. I'm going to approach. You can put your hands down, but don't move."

Heidi did as instructed, feeling like a child being scolded in school. As the DS approached, she saw that he wasn't in the full suit from earlier that day. He was in a plain t-shirt, and suit trousers though it looked as though they'd been pulled on hastily, with no belt, and his smart black shoes were unlaced.

"You were at home," she commented, seeing this.

"Yes I was! It's the middle of the night!"

"How did you even know I was here?! Do you have motion sensors set up in the shop?" she asked excitedly.

"No! You were seen! We had four separate calls about a suspicious individual breaking into this shop!"

Heidi felt herself colour and was glad that they were only lit by phone torches. She turned hers a little away but he shifted his to compensate and she was hit with a full beam of light to her scarlet face.

"I'm guessing you don't do much breaking and entering," he commented with a smirk.

"I didn't *break* anything!" she snapped.

"Alright. Fair point. Why did you illegally gain entrance to this property in the middle of the night without breaking anything?" he asked.

Heidi squirmed at the words, but held his gaze.

"To see if Lydia was murdered here."

"What?!"

Whatever answer he had been expecting, that clearly

wasn't it. He'd dropped his guard and looked suddenly younger. Heidi wondered again whether this might be his first big case.

"I thought she might have been," she told him with a shrug.

"Why?"

It was a simple enough question, and Heidi appreciated that he wasn't rejecting the suggestion out of hand, but she wasn't sure how much she should say. She didn't want to point the finger at Mary, or anyone else for that matter, without evidence.

"It's possible, isn't it? There wasn't much blood in the bookshop, at least not that I could see. Maybe she was killed somewhere else and placed in the bookshop afterwards."

"Why? Why the bookshop? Why move the body at all?"

"Well... if someone killed her in their own shop, they would need to move her somewhere else, right?" she ventured.

"Yes," he agreed slowly, clearly unconvinced.

"Or maybe the killer wanted to confuse things. To mess up your investigation," she suggested.

He looked even less convinced now.

"Why *your* shop? Why leave the body there?"

It was a good question. A very good question. Why

and how? If the killer was someone else, someone that had nothing to do with the break-ins, how had they got access to the bookshop, and why leave Lydia's body there?

Heidi deflated with a sigh.

"You're right. It doesn't make sense. It must have been the thief. No one else has access to the bookshop," she admitted glumly.

"I'm not saying that! We can't assume anything right now! I just wanted to know the reasoning that brought you out cat-burglaring in the middle of the night."

She gave him a dark look but let it go. After all, she didn't have much moral high-ground to balance on right now and her position was feeling decidedly precarious.

"There are a number of ways that people can gain access to a locked property. You need to invest in some better security. Better locks, maybe cameras, a decent alarm. The whole street needs upgrading. None of the shops are secure enough," he told her, "but that still doesn't answer the question. Even if someone could get into your shop, why? Why leave a body *there*?"

Chapter 8

"I almost got arrested."

"What?!" Maggie squawked in panic.

"I didn't though!" Heidi repeated, trying to be placating.

"Arrested?! What did you do?!"

"I... gained entry to Luscious Whisper to look around," Heidi admitted.

"Gained entry? What does that mean exactly?" Maggie demanded, cutting straight to the point.

"I went in through a back window."

"Heidi Cross! What on earth were you thinking?!"

Heidi winced but tried to remain firm.

"I wanted to check something out! How else was I supposed to do it?!" she protested.

"What? What did you want to check out? What was so important that you had to break into a closed shop? Practically a *crime scene*!"

"I *didn't* break anything!" Heidi argued, impatient at having to make this distinction again. DS Elliot hadn't seemed to see the significance the previous night, and Maggie looked just as unimpressed now, standing with her arms crossed, looking at Heidi like she were a naughty child.

"Breaking and entering is more than smashing glass and destroying padlocks."

Heidi grumbled a little at this, but it was clearly a losing battle.

"Besides," she began, trying to shift the focus of the conversation, "I thought that Luscious Whisper might actually *be* a crime scene."

It worked. Maggie was distracted. The crossed arms fell to her sides and she took an eager step forward.

"A crime scene? What crime?!"

"The murder! I thought that maybe Lydia was killed there and only placed in the bookshop after the fact," she explained excitedly.

"Why though? Why the bookshop?"

"I don't know. Or at least, I don't know why the bookshop specifically, but I can think of a few reasons to move a dead body," Heidi explained.

"To move suspicion away from the real killer!" Maggie declared, raising one finger to point at the sky in victory.

"That's one reason. A good reason!"

"What's another?"

"Maybe so that the crime scene can stay open?" Heidi suggested tentatively.

She watched as Maggie worked this out, following her train of thought to the same conclusion.

"You're talking about Mary," she said sadly.

Heidi's only response was a despondent shrug.

"Not just Mary though," Maggie added thoughtfully.

"What?"

"Well, we know that Mary is desperate to get back into her shop, and get access to everything about the business, but she's not the only one who would want their business to stay open," Maggie pointed out thoughtfully.

"You mean, if she was killed in a different shop entirely, the owner would still not want their business to close because of it?" Heidi queried.

"Exactly. Rent isn't cheap! Some of the businesses in the street must be struggling to make ends meet. Shutting their doors for a murder investigation would drive them under!"

"Especially if they're the killer," Heidi added drily.

"Quite. Did you find any evidence that Lydia was killed on her own premises?"

"None," Heidi admitted grudgingly.

DS Elliot had surprised her by walking through the shop with her, looking for blood stains, splatter or any other signs of violence. They hadn't found a thing, but

Heidi had appreciated being allowed to look for herself.

"So not worth getting arrested," Maggie commented.

"Well I *didn't* get arrested, so that's fine, isn't it."

"*Why* didn't you get arrested?" Maggie asked abruptly.

"I'm sorry?! Did you *want* me arrested?"

"Of course not dear, don't be silly, but it wouldn't have been an overreaction exactly, would it? You broke in through a window, to a locked shop! In the middle of the night! Why on earth are you walking around this morning, free as a bird?!"

Heidi had no answer to this question. In her own mind she hadn't been doing anything wrong, but in the harsh light of day she was prepared to admit that her actions had been foolish and in fact, highly illegal. Why wasn't she in trouble?

"You haven't charmed the handsome young Detective Sergeant, have you darling?" Maggie asked coyly.

Heidi flushed and shook her head quickly, casting the notion off.

"Don't be ridiculous!" she snapped.

"What's ridiculous about it?" Maggie asked curiously.

Heidi floundered.

"He's a policeman! He's- he's investigating a crime! He's not even thinking about- I mean, I'm sure he's-"

"Quite right," Maggie cut in, obviously taking pity on her, "I'm sure he just has other things to think about right now. He's looking for a murderer, not a burglar."

"Yes! Yes, exactly!" Heidi agreed gratefully.

"Still it's a shame. If he was enamoured with you, it would almost certainly help with our investigation," Maggie commented thoughtfully.

"Investigation?!" Shelley cried in despair. She had halted ten foot away and clearly wasn't coming any closer.

"Hello dear!" Maggie called cheerfully, ignoring Shelley's obvious distress.

"You're not still investigating Lydia's death are you?!" Shelley demanded, still rooted to the spot in the middle of the street.

"Keep your voice down, dear," Maggie admonished, casting a look up and down the cobbles.

No one was around to hear them, there was a definite lull in the usual hustle and bustle since the murder. They'd sold a scant dozen used books the day before and a Monday was likely to be even quieter.

Shelley reluctantly joined them, giving them both distinctly wary looks.

"We're not causing any trouble!" Maggie insisted, giving Heidi a warning wink, that clearly told her not to mention her night-time escapades and her brush with law enforcement.

"You better not be! I saw Jane and Charles Bingley on the way here and Jane was explaining all about you being cursed!"

"What?!" Heidi exclaimed in surprise.

"That's the word on the street! Everyone is saying it!" Shelley told her, "so you'd be better off staying away from the whole murder!"

"The body was in *my* bookshop! The murder came to *me*!" Heidi retorted.

"Yes dear, I gather that that's actually what's making people uncomfortable," Maggie commented, giving her a sympathetic pat on the shoulder.

"It's doesn't mean I'm cursed! But it makes it very hard to stay away from the whole thing!" Heidi explained in exasperation.

"Well of course you're not cursed, you don't need to tell me that. I've known you all your life and I'm still kicking aren't I?" Maggie soothed.

"But people are scared, and it's making them superstitious. It won't be good for business," Shelley pointed out.

"No. Very true. People won't want to come and browse the romance section if they think they might be struck down where they stand. No one wants to die with a bodice ripper in their hand! Though actually, I think that's exactly how I'd like to go," Maggie finished thoughtfully.

"I'd rather be reading something a bit more dignified," Shelley countered.

"Moby Dick? Or maybe something by Sir Arthur Conan Doyle," Maggie suggested.

"I'd want to be reading Agatha Christie," Heidi told them confidently.

"Christie? Really? She was an exceptional writer I suppose. And an exceptional woman too."

"It's what Joan was reading," Heidi told them, keeping her voice light.

"When she passed?" Shelley asked tentatively.

"Hm. She was just sitting in her chair reading and..." Heidi trailed off and an awkward silence descended.

"Which novel?" Maggie asked after a tense moment.

"Cat Amongst The Pigeons."

"Oh a cracker! Good for her!" Maggie exclaimed cheerfully.

"I haven't read it, is it good?" Shelley asked.

Just like that, the spell was broken. While Maggie offered heartfelt endorsement for one of her favourite Agatha Christies, Heidi counted her breaths, revelling in the feeling of calm.

It had been a terrible shock, but Maggie was right, it was a great book, by a splendid writer. They might not have seen it coming, but that didn't change the fact that it was exactly how Joan would have wanted to go.

"Miss Heidi Cross?"

All three heads swivelled.

"DS Elliot!" Heidi exclaimed, flushing as she felt Maggie's eyes on her.

"Nice to see you again," he said with a smile that drew a dimple to one cheek.

"Yes- I-" Heidi stammered incoherently, not having any clue as to the correct thing to say in this situation. Clearly he was making a teasing reference to the events of the night before, but should she respond in kind? Take umbrage? Ignore it entirely?

"And Maggie and Shelley, wasn't it? How are you both?" he asked, turning to the other two and sparing Heidi her agony of indecision.

"I'm very well, thank you! Though I'd like to know when the shop can re-open!" Maggie announced, taking charge of the conversation through brute force.

"That's just what I was coming to tell you actually. The bookshop can open tomorrow."

"Tomorrow?!" Heidi exclaimed in surprise.

"Does that mean you've caught the killer?!" Shelley asked eagerly.

"Ah. No, no it doesn't mean that unfortunately. We are still investigating and I have every confidence that the guilty party will be apprehended, but our investigation of the crime-scene has been completed." He reeled off the explanation as though he'd memorised it from a book.

"You're still sure the bookshop is a crime-scene?" Heidi pressed.

"At this time we have no reason to think otherwise," he replied firmly.

"What about the fact that I'm cursed?!" Heidi suggested frantically.

"I'm sorry?"

It was an idea that had sprung to her mind, fully formed. Possibly it was prompted by their discussion of Agatha Christie.

"There was a Christie novel, one of the Miss Marples, where a body was planted in the study of a manor house, just to throw off the investigation. The killers knew that a pretty, blonde dead girl in the study of a rich land-owner was a much more exciting story and would distract everyone from the truth!" she explained.

"I'm not sure I follow," DS Elliot admitted with a frown.

"Well, Lydia's body was found in my book shop. Now there's a rumour that I'm cursed and that's why Lydia is dead in my shop. That's a much more exciting story than the truth! Maybe that was the intention!"

He studied her thoughtfully.

"Why would anyone think you're cursed?"

Heidi flushed again. She couldn't help it. While she

willed her blood to recede, Maggie stepped into the breach for her.

"Because people are immensely foolish." she snapped.

"And a bit cruel, really," Shelley added quietly.

"But how would the killer have gained entrance to the bookshop?" DS Elliot asked, shaking his head.

"I can't answer *everything* for you! Besides, how did the killer get in anyway? Whether they killed her there or not? You're completely sure it was the thief, aren't you." Heidi surmised.

"It does seem to be the most likely explanation."

"Well I'm relieved," Shelley told them with a slight chuckle, "I was worried it was going to be one of the ladies competing for the attention of Mr Bingley!"

Slowly, they all turned to look at her, two pairs of eyes widening in excitement and one narrowing in confusion.

"Of course!" Maggie exclaimed.

"I didn't even think of that!" Heidi added.

"Who is Mr Bingley and what are you talking about?" DS Elliot demanded.

"I thought you were local," Heidi sighed in obvious disgust.

"I am! That doesn't mean I know all the *gossip*!" he argued, "wait, how did you know I was local?!"

"Well, you got here so quickly after I called about the

murder, and again last night," she mumbled, "and you'd clearly come from home in a rush."

She was surprised to see that he was smiling at her and shifted awkwardly from foot to foot.

"So tell me about this Mr Bingley then. Fill me in on all the gossip. Is there really a motive for murder here?"

"DS Elliot! Of course there is! A good man is hard to come by!" Maggie announced in scandalised tones, as though the very idea of considering Mr Bingley not worth killing for, were sacrilege.

"But who would *murder* for him?" Heidi asked Maggie, her expression thoughtful "who's the most desperate?"

"Well that's not how I would choose to phrase it," Maggie criticised.

"Who's the most romantic?" Heidi suggested uncertainly.

"I don't think that's right either!" Shelley was quick to comment.

"Alright, who's the most... invested in the idea of Charles Bingley?" Heidi offered, looking hopeful.

"Much better!" Maggie congratulated her, "I'd say that's Kitty, wouldn't you?"

"She did have the idea of a party first," Heidi agreed.

"And she did invite him to dinner," Shelley added despondently.

"Everyone was interested in him of course, but most of the ladies were more reserved about it. Elizabeth and Jane for instance- their behaviour was impeccable!" said Maggie.

"Are you really suggesting this as a motive?" DS Elliot cut in incredulously.

"I was only joking, but he is very handsome," Shelley added glumly.

"And so successful! He just opened an artisinal gin distillery in the street!" Maggie tacked on.

"He's kind too," Shelley added, keen to make this point clear.

"And there has been a fuss ever since he arrived. He's why Lydia threw that party the night she died," Heidi told him.

"She threw him a party?" DS Elliot asked somewhat incredulously.

"He's *very* handsome," Maggie repeated.

"And his business partner was here too. He was a bit of a mystery so everyone was excited to meet him."

"He's even richer than Charles Bingley, and he's handsome too I suppose, but he was kind of horrible," Shelley commented.

"Really? I saw him being horrible to Lydia, but I left just after that," Heidi interposed.

"He was horrible to everyone really, except Charles,"

Shelley told her with a shrug.

"I could almost forgive him for it if he put Lydia in her place, though I suppose I shouldn't say that now," Maggie noted thoughtfully.

"They had an altercation of some sort?" DS Elliot asked quickly, pulling out his notebook and pen.

"Not an altercation exactly, he was just a bit... off with her," Heidi explained. She gave as detailed an account as she could of the conversation between Mr Darcy and Lydia, and DS Elliot wrote it all down.

"She had no luck with Charles Bingley either. If she thought her party was going to win his affections, she was much mistaken!" Maggie crowed.

"Did they argue too?"

"No, she just failed to seduce him. She cut in when Kitty invited him to dinner, and she undermined every woman he spoke to, but he didn't fall for her tricks," Maggie explained triumphantly.

"No, I think he was keen on Jane though, don't you?" Shelley asked excitedly.

"Jane? Kitty? Exactly how many women did Miss Wickes insult and aggravate at the party?!"

The three women exchanged looks before answering in unison.

"All of them."

DS Elliot pressed a finger and thumb to the bridge of

his nose in obvious distress.

"Alright, start giving me names and details," he ordered, adjusting his grip on his notebook in readiness.

Shelley blanched at the thought but Maggie set to it with gusto. She gave names, backgrounds and as much detail as she could about arguments that Lydia had engaged in and jibes and taunts that she had made. Heidi listened with interest. It seemed that Lydia had been in fine form after Heidi had left, crossing women left and right. She'd been present for a comment about Kitty drinking, and of course she'd witnessed the argument with Rose, but Maggie reported an argument with Elizabeth and Jane too, as well as jibes and insults at a dozen more guests, and even a brief clash with Mary.

"Mary?!" Heidi exclaimed involuntarily when Maggie recounted the fact.

"That's Lydia's employee?" DS Elliot confirmed, giving Heidi an enquiring look.

"Yes, that is- she's the boss now, Lydia apparently left the business to her, but she was an employee."

DS Elliot's eyebrows shot up at this- a fact that Heidi couldn't help but notice.

"What?" she demanded.

"Hm?"

He quickly smoothed his brow, but Heidi was sure of what she'd seen.

"You just reacted to that. You were surprised. Are you thinking it gives Mary a motive? Or was it more than that?" she pressed on unrelenting.

"What do you mean?" he squirmed, taking a full step back.

"Did Lydia not leave Mary the business?"

He took another step back.

"Who did she leave the business to?!" Heidi demanded.

This direct assault was too much for DS Elliot, who clearly regretted having facial expressions altogether, and took another step back, colliding with a figure behind him.

"Oh! I'm sorry!" he cried, spinning around.

A completely white faced Mary stood motionless in the street behind him. She looked as though she were in shock.

"I just came to ask about... but- did she really not leave me the shop?" she stammered, her voice weak.

DS Elliot didn't answer, he just looked panicked.

"But she promised!" Mary told him imploringly.

"I'm so sorry, I can't disclose any information, Ms Wickes' lawyer will need to-" he began, but Mary fled. She was gone in an instant, running back up the street, slipping on the cobbles in her patent leather shoes.

DS Elliot rounded on Heidi with a look of intense irritation.

"That is absolutely *not* how that exchange should have gone! She needs to talk to the lawyer about issues of inheritance, not me!"

"That's not my fault, you should have practised beforehand!" Heidi snapped back.

"Practised?!"

"And I was right, wasn't I?! Lydia didn't leave the business to Mary!"

"I can't confirm that!"

Heidi took these words as absolute confirmation.

"Maggie you were right, Lydia lied to her," she commented, giving the older woman her due.

"I knew that snake couldn't be trusted. Poor Mary!" she exclaimed shaking her head.

"But at least that means Mary had no motive to kill her!" Shelley suggested happily.

"No it doesn't. Mary clearly thought she would inherit, so she still had motive either way," Heidi countered flatly.

"How can you seriously suspect her?! Or Rose or Robert or anyone?!" Shelley cried, flopping down unhappily into a chair.

""Why do you suspect Rose?!" DS Elliot asked quickly, setting his anger aside.

"Oh! She's the one who inherits then?" Heidi asked astutely.

"What?!" DS Elliot barked.

"Well it makes sense I suppose, most people would leave their business to their child," Heidi admitted.

"But she's never had any interest in the place!" Maggie said.

"Maybe she will now it's hers," Heidi suggested with a shrug.

"I didn't say that she inherits!" DS Elliot reminded them.

"Well, not *exactly*, but it was clear from the way you said it," Heidi told him.

"From the way I said *what*?!"

Heidi waved this question aside and turned back to Maggie.

"Do you think Rose knew? Inheriting could be motive aside from anything else," she asked.

"Aside from *what* else?" DS Elliot tried to cut in.

"If she did, that would be terribly heartless. Somehow I'd rather she'd killed for love than for personal gain," Maggie replied.

"I still think Robert is more likely anyway," Heidi told her.

"Do you think *he* knew she would inherit? If they do get married, that could be motive for him too!"

"STOP!" DS Elliot roared.

Shelley looked relieved but Maggie and Heidi were

obviously affronted.

"Young man, that is no way to speak to ladies!" Maggie scolded, crossing her arms over her chest and fixing him with a dark glare.

"I'm sorry. I am, I'm sorry, but you can't be theorising about potential murderers! You can't break into crime scenes! This could be very dangerous! *I* will find the killer, you need to stay out of it and let me!"

Both women seemed to consider this and surprisingly it was Heidi who dismissed it first.

"Rubbish!" she exclaimed, "you don't even know these people! You didn't know Lydia! How are you going to catch her killer?!"

"With police work! It's literally my job!" he told her, almost laughing in exasperation.

"But until we told you, you didn't even know that Lydia was keeping Rose and Robert from getting married! You didn't know Lydia was insulting people in an attempt to seduce Charles Bingley! You didn't know she'd promised the business to Mary!" Heidi reeled off.

"But I did once you told me! Give me the information and let me figure out how it connects. Please," he implored.

Heidi sighed but found the look of desperation in DS Elliot's eyes hard to ignore.

"This is your first big case, isn't it," she asked him

ruefully.

"I don't see what that has to do with anything," he replied, colouring swiftly.

She sighed again.

"Alright. Fine. You have a notebook full of gossip now, and anything else we hear, we'll let you know. That's the best I can do," she told him.

She thought for a second he was going to argue, but instead his face broke into a broad grin.

"Alright. In that case, you'd better take my number."

Chapter 9

"Shelley. Don't move," Maggie whispered once the DS had departed. She was holding her hands up as though fixed in place.

Shelley obediently froze.

"What's happening?" she muttered out of the merest corner of her mouth.

"Heidi just exchanged numbers with a man. I can't be sure that this isn't some sort of dream, but if it is, I don't want to shatter it."

A smile tugged at Shelley's lips, but Heidi looked entirely unimpressed.

"I did not *exchange numbers*," she claimed, with dramatic air quotes.

"Oh darling, that is exactly what just happened," Maggie informed her, still in a hushed voice.

"I did not!"

"Do you have his number?" Maggie asked.

Heidi didn't answer.

"Does he have yours?" Maggie continued.

Still Heidi was silent.

"There has been an exchange of numbers. I'm just so glad that I was here to see it!" she finished in tones of ecstasy.

"It's not like that! It's for crime solving! It was in the interest of peace! Of law and order!" Heidi cried.

"I love that show!" Shelley chimed in, earning herself a glare from Heidi.

"Heidi dear, I have known you your entire life, I have worked at the shop for years. Decades in fact!" Maggie told her calmly.

"What's your point?"

"Even I don't have your mobile number."

"But- well- that's because- I- I-" Heidi blustered.

"It's alright, I'm not complaining, I'm just trying to demonstrate the significance of what just happened," Maggie explained, her arms raised placatingly.

"It's just that I don't use my phone as a phone!" Heidi told her, still feeling the need to justify herself, "I use the shop phone for that! It's the business number, so it's always made sense! I only use my mobile for my running app, and as a torch, or to tell the time! I don't even have any numbers in it!"

These words seemed to freeze her companions for real.

"You don't have any numbers?" Shelley asked her in

an odd voice.

"Well, I have the GP saved, and the optician..."

"Anyone who isn't a healthcare professional?" Maggie asked.

Heidi didn't know what to say. She was entirely used to thinking of her mobile phone as a sort of technological swiss army knife, rather than a communication device, but Shelley and Maggie were making her feel distinctly uncomfortable about it.

"Give it here!" Shelley snapped, sounding unusually forceful.

Heidi meekly handed it over.

"I'm saving my number! Maggie you save yours. You can't have a mobile with no numbers in! It's criminal!"

Maggie dutifully saved her own number, evidently tickled by Shelley's disapproval.

"There you are! Three numbers! Shelley, myself and the lovely DS Elliot!"

Before Heidi could argue against Maggie's obvious insinuations, a voice cut in.

"Ah! Second hand books! Such a joy!"

Heidi almost winced. Mr Price always seemed to be performing for the people at the back, projecting his voice in a way that made Heidi feel far too conspicuous for comfort.

"Alexander!" Maggie trilled happily.

"Maggie, my dear, you look ravishing as ever!" he boomed.

He actually bent and kissed her hand, a move that made even the somewhat dramatic Maggie look uncertain.

"How are you ladies this fine day?" he asked solicitously, including Shelley and Heidi and possibly the whole street in the question with one sweeping gesture of his arm.

"Good thank you, Mr Price. We just found out that the bookshop can open," Shelley told him brightly.

"Really? Have the police said something then?" he asked quickly, his manner faltering as his interest rose to the fore.

"Just that they've got everything they can from the scene of the crime," Maggie told him with a dainty shrug.

"No suspects? No theories?" he probed.

"Too many," Shelley replied darkly.

At Mr Price's raised eyebrow, Maggie chuckled.

"Shelley can't bear to think of anyone as a suspect!" she explained.

"I don't know how you can! We know all these people! How can you think that Kitty or Jane or anyone would kill Lydia over Charles Bingley?! Or that Rose would hurt her own mother to inherit her shop?!"

"Because someone *did* kill Lydia," Heidi told her gently, "it already happened. It seems unthinkable, but clearly someone *did* think it. Now we just need to know who."

Shelley was clearly not comforted by this way of looking at things. She seemed unprepared to accept Lydia's murder as proof that there was a murderer in their midst. Heidi sighed but she didn't think there was anything she could say that would make a difference.

"What else can you tell me about the blackmail?" she asked Mr Price, turning her attention to him.

"The blackmail? What does that have to do with scorned lovers or inheritance?" he asked in surprise.

"We don't know why Lydia was killed. We can't neglect a single possibility!" Maggie declared.

"Well I'm afraid I can't be much help. For obvious reasons, people are reluctant to provide any particulars. You'd best speak to the victims directly!" he suggested.

Heidi frowned. It was easier said than done, particularly when everyone thought you were cursed.

"Could you look after the bookstall yourselves?" Heidi asked Maggie.

"Why?! What are you going to do?!" Shelley demanded.

"Of course dear!" Maggie cut in, ignoring Shelley completely.

"DS Elliot wanted you to leave it to him!" Shelley

implored.

"Nonsense," Maggie told her, waving away this notion like a fly, "you go and do some investigating Heidi, dear. See what you can find out. They might not want to tell you what they're being blackmailed about, but they might still show you any notes or threats, and that would be a start!"

Heidi squared her shoulders and set off down the road with purpose. This sense of noble intention carried her all the way to the door of Jane and Elizabeth's clothing shop, but faltered as she crossed the threshold. It wasn't particularly busy, being a weekday, but there was still a fair number of people mooching around, scanning the shelves and looking at dresses and tops. Heidi noted how different the atmosphere was from that of Luscious Whisper. Where the lingerie shop was all black and chrome, with dark red velvet and shadowy alcoves, this clothing shop, just a few doors away, was filled with light and colour. The scrubbed wood floors were decorated with bright rugs and the white walls made the beautiful, vibrant clothes pop. Still, from the moment she set foot inside, Heidi felt almost overwhelmingly ill-at-ease. It wasn't just that she hadn't been clothes shopping in years; it wasn't even that she never felt comfortable in unfamiliar surroundings.

It was Elizabeth.

She was watching Heidi through narrowed,

suspicious eyes from behind the counter. She seemed to be studying her every move as though she were a shoplifter.

Heidi could only handle a few seconds before it was too much. She approached the till and summoned up a smile, trying to look natural and curse-free.

"Hi! Your shop is lovely!" she told Elizabeth sincerely. The woman didn't thaw even a little.

"Why are you here?"

"Maybe I'm shopping," Heidi replied, flustered.

"You've never been in here before," Elizabeth pointed out flatly.

"Well, I have all my mum's clothes," Heidi explained.

She knew instantly that it was a mistake. The mentioned of her deceased mother was just one more piece of evidence in the argument that she was indeed cursed. Elizabeth took an involuntary step back and almost collided with a display of jewellery on the back wall.

"You seriously think that Lydia died because of me?!" Heidi hissed under her breath, "what, did I eat a poisoned apple that I don't know about?! This is ridiculous!"

Elizabeth at least had the good sense to look abashed and she coloured to the roots of her dark curls.

"Well what do *you* think happened?!" she challenged, keeping her voice low.

"I think someone stabbed her with a bloody great knife! I don't have any idea why she was in my shop, but I don't think there's anything mystical or magical about it! It's more likely that the same person who's been stealing from all of us, getting into our shops undetected in the night, is the same one who killed her!"

Heidi's voice had risen as she spoke, and Elizabeth was looking nervously at her patrons, clearly worried about scaring them away.

"Yes alright, alright, but that doesn't explain why you're *here*!"

Heidi sighed and intentionally dropped her voice down to a whisper.

"I'm told you're being blackmailed."

Elizabeth's whole body tensed.

"Who- it doesn't matter. It's nothing." she snapped.

"Blackmail is rarely nothing," Heidi pointed out.

"I'm not telling you anything! We're handling it! Just butt out!" she hissed.

Heidi's pulse quickened at Elizabeth's twisted, snarling expression. Her instinct was to turn and run, but she stood her ground, remembering what Maggie had told her.

"I don't want to know what you're being blackmailed about. That's none of my business."

Elizabeth relaxed very slightly, her expression losing some of it's fierceness.

"What then?" she asked warily.

"How does it work? Were you sent a note? Do you still have it?" Heidi asked.

"It was left on the counter when we came in one morning," she explained, gesturing to the currently empty space in front of her, beside the till.

"So it's definitely the same person who's been stealing," Heidi commented thoughtfully.

"I'd say so. They asked for money to be left out," Elizabeth told her with a hollow laugh, "as if we have any to spare!"

"Lizzie!" A voice called happily from the doorway as Jane swept in, wreathed in smiles.

"Jane!" Elizabeth started guiltily.

"Oh! Heidi!" Jane stopped in her tracks, the glow of her happiness dimming, but then she came forward purposefully.

"It's good to see you Heidi. I'm sorry I haven't stopped by to say how sorry I am for what you're going through."

Her voice was gentle but firm and Heidi really believed that she meant what she said. Still, that didn't mean that she or Elizabeth weren't viable suspects.

"Thank you. It was... awful," Heidi admitted with an uncomfortable shrug.

"Will the bookshop be able to open again soon? Have the police given you any idea?"

"Tomorrow actually."

Both women looked surprised but smothered their expressions quickly.

"Oh good! Hopefully that means they're making progress! I'll just go and put my jacket away and then you can go for your lunch Lizzie," Jane told them, disappearing off towards the back of the shop.

Elizabeth waited until she was gone and then slid an envelope out of a draw beneath the till.

"Here," she said, "I already have it memorised. Maybe if you can figure out who it is, I wont have to find a way to come up with the money."

Elizabeth's tone was resigned rather than hopeful. She handed the envelope over to Heidi with a sad smile. Heidi slipped it into her pocket and was gone before Jane came back.

"Well?" Maggie asked excitedly as Heidi collapsed back into her chair at the used book stall. The street was empty, without even the usual trickle of students meandering in their free time.

"They definitely think I'm cursed."

Shelley sighed, as though this was exactly the outcome that she had expected, but Maggie waved the words away.

"Never mind that! Did she tell you anything about

the blackmail?!"

"The note was left inside the shop when they came in one morning. It must be the thief, unless there are *two* creeps able to get into locked shops at will," Heidi reported.

"Did they keep the note?! Did they let you see it?!" Maggie urged.

"I don't think Jane knows, but Elizabeth gave it to me. It sounds like the payment deadline hasn't passed yet. I think she's hoping we'll figure out who it is before she has to worry about coming up with the money."

"I expect she's already worrying about it. If I was her I'd be worrying about nothing else," Maggie commented darkly.

"Maybe they wont have to pay anyway!" Shelley cut in hopefully, "if it was the blackmailer who killed Lydia, maybe they're gone! Maybe they've run away!"

Maggie and Heidi considered this. Had anyone suddenly vanished? Were any shopfronts suddenly lifeless? Anyone conspicuously absent?

"It's so quiet, it's hard to tell, but, is anyone gone from the street?" Heidi asked, looking up and down the road helplessly.

"I don't know," Maggie admitted, also surveying the vast expanse of empty cobbles. A single tourist exited the clothes shop and hurried away, glancing to their left and right, clearly aware of the tension in the air.

"Maggie, maybe you should check. You know, you could stop in the businesses and see if everyone is still here," Heidi suggested.

"I suppose I could do the rounds- make sure everyone is accounted for," she replied importantly.

"But first-" Heidi said, halting her.

She carefully pulled out the note, first studying the envelope. It was plain white, but not the correct size for a letter. It was more like the type of envelope that comes with a greeting card. There was no visible watermark or anything of that kind, and no name had been written on the front. When Heidi opened it, she found a folded piece of paper. It didn't match the size of the envelope and she had to take a moment to picture how she would have folded the paper herself, to create a better fit.

"Well?!" Maggie nudged her impatiently.

"Sorry,"

Heidi slid the piece of paper free and unfolded it. She wasn't sure what she had expected but she found herself initially underwhelmed.

"Is that it?" Maggie asked, clearly feeling much the same way.

The note read-

I found the box in the back room.

You should be more careful with your secrets.

£1000 on the desk on the last day of the month by midnight.

Or everyone will know.

Heidi read the note through three times, soaking in the words.

"How horrible!" Shelley whispered, her fingers pressed to her lips.

"It's just typed!" Maggie complained.

"Yes..." Heidi agreed thoughtfully.

"What's wrong with that?" Shelley asked, confused.

"If it was handwritten, we could look for a writing match. If it was letters from magazines and newspapers we could figure out which publications and maybe there would be something there but... I think we'd need to check a specific printer or computer or something to find out if it created this note," Heidi explained.

"Well yes," Maggie agreed, "this is true of course, but I actually meant- well- it's not very exciting is it?! Letters cut from a magazine would have been much better!"

"Like a proper villain," Shelley agreed, nodding solemnly.

"Still, I suppose this would have been an awful shock for the girls, especially coming out of nowhere!"

"What do you think was in the box in the back room?" Shelley asked guiltily, clearly uncomfortable but

159

still curious.

"I don't know, and I said I wouldn't ask," Heidi told them firmly.

"Good for you dear!" Maggie congratulated her, "we can of course theorise though! Maybe it's explicit pictures! Or stolen goods!"

"Stolen goods?! You think they've committed a crime?!" Shelley asked, aghast.

"I'm sure I couldn't say, but it needs to be something pretty serious if the blackmailer expects them to pay up."

"A thousand pounds. It's an odd amount. Isn't it?" Heidi queried.

"In what way? Too high or too low?" Maggie asked.

"Well both, really. It's not a huge amount in the scheme of things, but it's a lot to Jane and Elizabeth. I got the impression that they really might not be able to pay it. Do you think the blackmailer knew not to ask for more than that?"

"How could they know? How could they know what Jane and Elizabeth could afford?" Shelley asked, her posture tightening.

"They must know them pretty well. It must be someone who knows them well enough to know how their business is doing, and what their rent is, that sort of thing." Maggie suggested.

"Why do you keep insisting that it's someone we

know?! Someone we're friends with?!" Shelley cried.

"I'm sorry dear, but the evidence keeps pointing that way!" Maggie told her sympathetically.

"Or maybe the blackmailer went through their books? Snooped around the business? Calculated exactly how much money they might be able to afford?" Heidi offered, hoping to soothe Shelley's distress.

"What?! That's horrible! You think the blackmailer is breaking into all the shops and snooping and spying like that?!" Shelley remarked, horrified.

Since Shelley was clearly going to be unreasonable no matter what she said, Heidi didn't hazard a reply.

"The last day of the month..." Maggie read aloud.

"Yep. Not far off," Heidi noted.

"Think we'll have it all sorted in time?"

Heidi almost laughed until she realised that Maggie was serious. She really believed that they could solve a murder in a matter of days.

"Maybe," she settled on, after a moment's pause.

It would be nice if they could. She remembered the strain in Elizabeth's face and the genuine sympathy in Jane's. It would be really nice to find the blackmailer in time.

"So what's next?" Maggie asked, clearly ready to get going and make headway.

"Well you can start checking in to see if anyone is gone," Heidi reminded her.

"And you?"

"I don't really know," she admitted with a sigh.

"What suspects do we have? What clues are there? What could you follow up on?" Maggie pressed.

"I suppose... I could talk to Kitty. I want to know how determined she was to get close to Charles Bingley, and how far she would have gone to get Lydia out of her way. It sounds as though she was being blackmailed too, and I should check that it was the same person as was blackmailing Elizabeth and Jane. Maybe there's a clue in there somewhere. I want to find out more about Lydia's ex-husband too, but I'm not sure how to go about it."

Maybe start with a search on the computer?" Maggie suggested vaguely.

"Well I think you're both crazy," Shelley told them in exasperation.

"Crazy for wanting to find the killer in our midst?!"

"Yes! The whole thing is mad, and DS Elliot is going to be furious when he realises you're still investigating," she told them.

"I suspect we'll get away with it actually, so long as we keep him updated," Maggie countered with a smile and a glance at Heidi.

"I guess you'll find out, won't you. Are you planning

to open the shop tomorrow Heidi? Now that you've got permission?"

"Oh! Yes- yes I suppose there's no reason not to. It's not like we're shifting any of these second hand books, with no one out in the street to even see them."

"Business will pick up again," Maggie assured her, "once this is all sorted out things will get back to normal, you just wait and see."

Chapter 10

Maggie hustled off to start accosting their neighbours and
Shelley agreed to man the deserted book stall by herself
while Heidi went to find Kitty. The flower shop kept
regular hours and Kitty ran the place single handed, so if it
was open, Heidi should be able to talk to her without her
running off. The shop looked open from the outside. The
sign on the door welcomed her in, but as she pushed it
open she was seized by doubt. The air was cool and she
shop itself was shady. With the bouquets, potted plants
and floral arrangements all around the walls it felt like
stepping into the woods, except for one thing.

It was silent.

No bird song, no leaves rustling in the breeze and no
Kitty.

"Hello?" Heidi called tentatively.

There was no answer. She stepped further in, edging
around a large monstera plant, and called out again but
still there was no reply.

"Kitty? Are you here?"

She made her way toward the back of the shop where the cash desk stood, and stopped abruptly, her heart racing and her stomach heaving. She was frozen in place while her mind screamed at her to run. How could this be happening?! Again?! Kitty lay sprawled on the floor, face down. Heidi could almost see the knife handle protruding from her back, except that she couldn't. There was no knife handle there. Her feet carried her forward against her will and she crouched down beside Kitty's prone form. Reaching out one hand, she grasped her wrist. It was warm! And- there! There was a pulse!

All at once it was as though the world screamed in around Heidi. She was no longer frozen inside her own body, no longer nauseous, no longer afraid.

"Kitty? Are you hurt?" she asked quickly, kneeling over the young woman and trying to turn her. As she lifted her dead weight, she was hit by a wave of sharp, pungent odour. Kitty reeked of alcohol. It was coming off her in clouds, making Heidi feel instantly queasy again.

"Kitty?" Heidi asked louder, shifting the woman onto her side.

Her face was pale and shiny with sweat and Heidi was on the verge of calling an ambulance when she stirred slightly and muttered quietly,

"I'll be right with you! One peace lily coming up!"

With a sigh Heidi stood up and looked around. She

had no idea what to do in this situation, she'd never been drunk herself and had never seen either of her parents or Joan this way either. This was something new and she didn't know how best to handle it. Pulling out her phone she did a quick search online and found lots of recommendations for water, painkillers and the recovery position. Nothing covered this exact scenario, but she supposed she'd just have to do her best and play it by ear.

First up, water and painkillers. There must be some around here somewhere. Heidi stepped around the counter and through the back door into a work room. There was a huge industrial fridge, filled with flowers, and instead of a kitchenette, a workbench and sink. The cupboards were all filled with ribbon and twine rather than drinking glasses and medicines, but eventually Heidi found a mug that smelled of vodka. She washed it thoroughly, until the last vestiges of the smell had faded, and set it to drain as she continued her hunt. The tiny watercloset yielded positive results. There was barely room for a minute sink opposite the toilet but on the cistern Heidi found a whole stack of paracetamol, ibuprofen and aspirin. She grabbed a box of each, filled the mug with water and returned to Kitty, still curled on the floor.

"Kitty, do you think you could sit up and drink some water?" she asked uncertainly.

Kitty still looked dead to the world and Heidi

doubted that she'd even heard her, but then she tipped and rolled slightly in a movement that could just about be considered to be nodding. Heidi had to lift her up and support her weight by crouching beside her with one arm around her, but she was able to get the cup to her lips and Kitty took a few sips. Heidi pressed an ibuprofen to her lips and Kitty obediently took it with another few sips of water. She was just starting to slump against Heidi again when the sound of the shop door roused her, bringing panic to her eyes. She tried desperately to scramble up but her body wouldn't hold her intention and she flailed and slumped anew.

"It's OK, it's OK!" Heidi whispered.

"I'll be right with you!" she called louder, to the shop at large.

She hooked one arm under each of Kitty's and dragged her through the door to the workroom, propping her against the wall with the water cup beside her. With a deep breath, she stepped back into the shop with a smile on her face, ready to greet and serve a customer despite knowing nothing whatsoever about flowers.

"You do house plants?" the woman asked cheerfully, still looking around the shop at the shelves and shelves of greenery.

"Yes! We have lots of house plants," Heidi agreed, her fingers crossed for luck behind the counter.

"Do you have anything low maintenance? Something easy to look after? I'd like to get something for my son's university room," the woman told her.

Heidi stepped over to the nearest shelf of potted plants, all of which looked spiky and entirely unlike the sort of plants that Heidi was used to. The label on the shelf said 'succulents' and Heidi was relieved to see a small card attached to each pot. She scanned it quickly and her smile relaxed into something more sincere.

"The card on each pot gives details on care and optimal conditions," she explained.

"Oh lovely! I'll have a look and pick out something I think he can manage!"

She opted for one of the succulents, since it seemed from the cards as though they could survive long periods of absolute neglect. It was probably a good choice for a dorm-room.

Heidi rang through her purchase and waved her off before slipping back to the workroom to check on Kitty. She'd slumped over onto the floor again, but she was lying on her side and it looked as though she'd drunk some more of the water first. Heidi found a jacket and wadded it up as a pillow, then returned to the shop to keep an eye out for more customers. It seemed she was going to be stuck there for a while.

Luckily it was a slow afternoon, with few customers

to challenge Heidi's knowledge of flora. She couldn't help noticing that it was substantially more people than had visited the book stall since the murder, but she chose to hold to the belief that Maggie was right, and once the case was solved business would pick back up.

Kitty remained between sleep and unconsciousness for a couple of hours, and Heidi used the time to snoop. It tugged at her conscience, but she was there to get information and she wasn't getting it from Kitty directly, so she had to be a little ruthless. The most significant discovery was a collection of bottles in the flower refrigerator. Clearly this was not Kitty's first time drinking at work, and it seemed as though it might be a full-blown problem. Heidi remembered Lydia making a comment about Kitty's drinking at the party, and her obvious embarrassment and distress. She wondered who else knew about it. It would obviously be a difficult secret to keep, but Heidi mixed so little usually that she'd been completely oblivious.

"If you're looking for the blackmail note, it's not here," a weary voice croaked as Heidi rummaged through a drawer in the workbench.

"Kitty! How are you feeling?"

"Awful. What time is it?" she struggled to sit up as she spoke, clutching her head.

"Almost five. You can probably leave and just close

the shop now, it's pretty quiet," Heidi told her.

"The shop is open?! But what- I-" she trailed off, frantic and helpless, her eyes filling with tears.

"I found you on the floor," Heidi told her, helping Kitty into a sitting position up against the wall and sitting down beside her, "I don't think anyone else saw you. I got you to the back here, and you've had some water and aspirin. I served any customers that came in. No one knew you were back here, no one saw anything."

Kitty sighed, long and low, her head hanging forward.

"Thank you."

"What happened?" Heidi asked gently.

Kitty was silent for a moment. It was clear that Heidi wasn't just asking about today.

"I don't really know. I used to have a glass of wine when I got upstairs after work at the end of the day. Then I started having it down here, before I went upstairs. Then it got earlier and earlier and stronger and stronger, until... it is really hard running a business alone! When things are good, it's more work than I can handle! More hours than I can fit in the day! And when things are bad... that's why I wanted to talk to Charles Bingley! I wanted advice on finding an investor!"

Heidi understood. It was a familiar struggle, that many of the shops in the street faced. Rents were high and business could be unpredictable. You could never be sure whether you were going to have a good month or a bad one and that fear alone took a toll.

"I don't think you should keep drinking," Heidi told her, cringing at the inadequacy of her own words.

"No," Kitty sighed, "I probably shouldn't. It's just... hard to stop once you've started. But I don't want to be this person. The idea of people seeing me falling down drunk is pretty unbearable. I thought I was so discrete about it too, until Lydia started making snide remarks. I must have been a real mess and I had no idea."

Tears were running down her face now and in lieu of something useful to do, Heidi refilled the cup of water.

"Thank you. You didn't have to help me, but you did," Kitty remarked as she sipped.

"Well I wasn't going to just leave you on the floor," Heidi told her.

"Some people would have."

"I think probably just Lydia," Heidi countered.

"True. She was such a cow."

Heidi couldn't exactly disagree. Lydia had worked out what was going on with Kitty, and instead of offering her help, or even just keeping her distance, she'd used the knowledge to undermine and humiliate her. Unfortunately it gave Kitty motive for murder.

"I didn't kill her," Kitty announced, as though she'd

read Heidi's thoughts.

An uneasy silence settled around them as Heidi struggled to think of what to say. Some response felt necessary but these were uncharted waters.

"I came home after the party. I was upstairs asleep, drunk. I know I can't prove that, but it's true. I was angry at Lydia, but I was more embarrassed and upset, I wasn't looking for revenge. And killing her wouldn't have kept my drinking a secret, because the blackmailer already knew about it. I got my first letter just over a month ago, and another last week."

"You got two?!" Heidi asked quickly.

"Yep. Asking for more money."

"Do you have the letters?"

"I still have the second one, but I tore up the first one after I paid. I didn't want to look at it any more, and I was hoping it was all over. I guess it's not."

She looked utterly defeated and Heidi felt a tight twisting in her chest.

"Could I see the letter you still have?" she asked.

"Sure. Help me upstairs and you can have it."

Between them they got Kitty onto her feet and once the shop was locked up and the computer shut down, Heidi supported her up the narrow staircase. It wasn't easy, but they made it to the top and after much fumbling with the key, Kitty managed to open the door and stumble

172

gratefully into her flat. Like Heidi she lived above her shop, though it was a smaller space, made even more cramped by the general chaos. Heidi looked around in poorly disguised horror, making Kitty wince.

"I know. Things have got out of control but... I'm going to get everything straightened out."

There was mess on every surface. Dirty plates littered the coffee table, crusted mugs sat discarded everywhere and the floor was strewn with clothing and rubbish. A still open bottle stood on a kitchen counter thick with grime.

"One minute," Kitty told her, slipping into another room, presumably her bedroom. She returned a moment later with a plain, though slightly stained envelope that matched the one Elizabeth and Jane had received. She pressed it into Heidi's hands and let go with some reluctance.

"You won't tell anyone?" she asked, glancing back at her flat.

"I won't but-"

"I'll sort it out. I will. I'm going to stop drinking and get my life back on track. I swear."

"Shall I take that with me?" Heidi asked, nodding to the bottle in the kitchen.

Kitty's eyes widened slightly, but after the briefest of hesitations she agreed. Heidi ended up leaving with a half a dozen bottles in a carrier bag.

"I'll be back for the ones downstairs first thing in the morning," she told Kitty, "and I know how many there are. I'm just saying..."

Kitty nodded, her expression fierce but unreadable, at least to Heidi.

"Thank you," she muttered, as Heidi made her way back downstairs.

Heidi nodded, but still wasn't sure what to say. In the end it was unnecessary. Kitty closed the door before Heidi had gone another step.

Chapter 11

Heidi was as good as her word the next morning. Although she wanted nothing more than to stay in her flat, hiding from the world, she set her iced coffee on the kitchen counter, left her breakfast in the fridge, and took a duffel bag with her across the road to the florist. At the sound of her gentle knock, Kitty came quickly to the door. She looked tired but clear eyed and Heidi gave her a small uncertain smile which Kitty returned.

"Thank you for this. I've left them in the fridge. I didn't want to touch them..." she trailed off, shaking her head and closing her eyes for a second.

"That's fine. I brought a bag this time, so no one will see even if they happen to be up this early. I'll get them out of here."

Heidi followed Kitty to the back and started loading the bottles carefully into the bag.

"That's alright actually. I've been thinking a lot since last night, and I think- I think it's fine if people know. I'm serious about quitting. I don't want to be this person any more, and I'll do whatever it takes to change. Besides, I bet most people already know. If Lydia figured it out, she won't have been the only one. And she made those comments at her party, so it's not exactly a secret any more anyway, is it?" she asked, her eyes glistening.

"Alright, well- I- I think that's good. It's good you've stopped drinking and good that you're not hiding it. People in the street are nice, they won't-" Heidi attempted, but broke off.

"Exactly," Kitty agreed with a wry smile.

"Exactly."

"I should never have started drinking in the first place. I should have known better. My mum could never drink without taking it too far and embarrassing herself. She used to make people cringe, stumbling around, and the things she would say! But I guess you live and learn," she finished with a shrug.

"I think people find it hard to learn lessons from their parents, there's too much baggage there," Heidi commented. She was thinking primarily of fictional characters but she supposed the insight still applied.

"Mothers and daughters is always a tense relationship," Kitty agreed, "Just look at Lydia and Rose."

"What do you mean?"

"Well Lydia was awful to her! Always! She was controlling and mean, all snide remarks and criticism. She hated Robert just on principal, because he made Rose happy."

"But, she left Rose the business! She must have loved her!" Heidi exclaimed.

"Of course she loved her, but that didn't stop her being awful," Kitty replied with a shrug.

Heidi couldn't help wondering whether her relationship with her own mother would have distorted in the same way, evolving over time into something bitter and sharp-edged.

"People are so confusing," she said, shaking her head slowly.

"They are. I didn't know Lydia had left Rose the business, I thought it was going to Mary. Does she know?"

"Mary knows, she sort of found out by accident," Heidi explained, blushing, "but I don't think Rose knows yet."

"I wonder what she'll do. I mean, it's not like you and the bookshop, is it? I don't think Rose has ever wanted Luscious Whisper.

Heidi felt the smallest pang, but pushed it aside.

"Maybe she'll sell it then?" she suggested, though to her the idea was unthinkable.

"It would certainly give her and Robert a leg up in life if she did! It's a really successful business! I'm surprised lingerie and kinky stuff is so popular with the Cambridge crowd, but it must be. I mean, that party alone must have cost her a chunk of cash and that wasn't even really for business reasons! She just wanted to impress Charles Bingley and meet the new guy. She must have been gutted when she realised she already knew him!"

"What? She already knew Mr Darcy?!" Heidi asked, surprised.

"Yeah! Didn't you know? They knew each other from way back, so he wasn't impressed by her fancy party or her showing off, he already hated her."

Heidi mulled this over. Mr Darcy had seemed to dislike Lydia, and there had been something strange between them that Heidi hadn't understood. It made sense if they already knew each other and had a negative history of some sort.

"How did they know each other?" she asked.

"No clue, sorry. I just heard them talking to each other. She told him he hadn't changed, and he said that she hadn't changed *enough*. I laughed which is probably why she went after me later in the evening."

"She went after everyone," Heidi consoled her.

"That shouldn't surprise me," Kitty sighed.

"She was pretty horrible wasn't she. Still- stabbed in the back seems a bit-"

"Excessive?" Kitty suggested.

"Exactly."

"Police are pretty sure it was the blackmailer?" Kitty asked.

"Seems that way. There are lots of possibilities, but the blackmailer had a way into the bookshop. No one else had that, so the blackmailer seems the most likely culprit."

"They have a way into the flower shop too," Kitty told her.

"They do? No break in?"

"Nope. Money was taken, and some orchids too, of all things. Then the blackmail note was just left on the counter, by the till. I'm not making another payment. I don't care what they do or who they tell about my drinking, I'm not paying another penny. I'll use the money I would have given them to change all the locks! I should have done that right away, but at first I wasn't sure it was really happening, you know? I've been losing track of things. I lost my keys for three days! So... I wondered if I had lost the money, or taken it myself. And when the note came, I was panicked. Stopping word getting out felt like the most important thing! But now, I'm ready to stand up for myself. I'm changing the locks and that's that. The blackmailer can go hang for all I care."

Heidi agreed with the sentiment, but she had just one small request to add to it.

"Do you think the lock change could wait?"

"Alright men! We need a full breakdown of information. Debriefing in t-minus five minutes!" Maggie called as she burst into the bookshop.

"What does t-minus five minutes mean?" Heidi asked, looking up from the desk where she had been going through the drawers, making sure the police hadn't moved anything.

"I'm not really sure to be honest. Shall we just do our debrief now? Mine is very simple if it helps at all- no one has vanished from the street since the murder. The guilty party has not absconded!"

"Not surprising really," Heidi sighed.

"It would have made things too simple anyway," Maggie told her breezily.

"That wouldn't necessarily be a bad thing you know. There is actually a killer lurking around! Finding out who they are is sort of the point."

"Yes yes, but a worthy adversary would make the whole thing much more satisfying, and would impress the lovely Detective Sergeant Elliot," Maggie pointed out.

As she spoke, the bell over the door chimed and they both spun around.

"Did I hear my name?"

DS Elliot stood in the doorway with a broad grin creating dimples on his cheeks. The effect was that he looked even younger but at the same time made Heidi blush furiously.

"DS Elliot! What a pleasant surprise!"

Heidi could hear the smile in Maggie's voice but she fixed her own gaze on the floor and clenched her teeth. She tried to relax, to play off the moment with humour, but she just couldn't do it.

"Do you have any updates for me? You didn't call," he asked, moving further into the shop, towards Heidi.

She tried to respond, to give any kind of answer at all, but she couldn't force the words out through her tightly clamped jaw.

"Heidi? Miss Cross?" He asked uncertainly, the dimples fading from his cheeks.

Shelley arrived, saving the day with her entrance, allowing Heidi the space to catch her breath.

"Morning all!" she called, "lovely to be back in the shop, isn't it!"

She cast only the briefest glance at the floor, noting one missing rug and moving swiftly past it.

"Good morning Shelley, dear. The Detective Sergeant is just paying us a visit, to see how the case is progressing. How are things going on your end?" she addressed this last to DS Elliot, forcing his attention away from the still silent Heidi.

"Um, well, there's not really much that I can disclose. It is an ongoing investigation," he hedged.

"Well that's not particularly fair! You expect *us* to share information!"

"I can't lay my whole case out for you, but if you have any particular questions I'll do my best to answer them, how about that?" he ventured, looking from Maggie to Heidi.

Heidi managed a small shrug and Maggie sighed theatrically.

"I suppose we can agree to those terms. Heidi was about to give me an update anyway, weren't you dear?" she asked just a little uncertainly.

"Yes I- I just need to run upstairs first. I'll be right back," Heidi assured them, bolting for the door to the stairs. She was up them in no time and safely inside her flat, breathing heavily.

What did she know? What did she know? What could she tell them?

She hadn't planned for this, she was just supposed to be talking to Maggie right now, telling her about Kitty's blackmail and anything else that came to mind. She wasn't ready to present her non-existent findings to a police officer! Especially not DS Elliot.

"Just breathe," her mother told her in a whisper, reaching out a hand that could never touch her.

Heidi did her best. In for three and out for four. Three. Four. Three. Four.

She quickly ran through things in her mind, and tried to put her thoughts in a logical order. She would just have to ignore Maggie's blatant insinuations and teasing, and present the facts.

She descended the stairs at a much more moderate pace and took one last deep breath before pushing the door open. The three of them were standing close together, talking in low voices that Heidi could make out with perfect clarity in the quiet of the shop.

"Did I do something wrong?" DS Elliot asked anxiously.

"No, no, it's just who she is. It's sad, she was such a confident, chatty little girl," Maggie told him, shaking her head sadly.

Heidi felt a simmering under her skin. Emotions clashed and mixed together. They were talking about her. They were stood together, literally critiquing her behaviour!

"What happened?" DS Elliot asked.

"EVERYBODY DIED."

They all spun to look at her in shock, and no wonder- she hadn't meant to but she'd practically shouted the words.

"Heidi, dear-" Maggie began, flushing furiously, but Heidi cut her off.

Shelley, wide eyed and pale, opened her mouth to

speak but Heidi didn't want to hear it.

"I spoke to Elizabeth and to Kitty. They were both being blackmailed. In both cases the blackmailer was able to get into their shop without breaking in. They were asked for money, but not so much that they couldn't afford to pay it. Kitty also told me that Lydia and Rose had a really difficult relationship. She thinks that Lydia hated Robert because he made Rose happy, so I think Robert still needs to be a suspect."

She fired off these facts with brutal efficiency, not waiting for feedback or response. Once she was finished she merely waited, looking blankly at her distinctly uncomfortable company.

"Gosh," Shelley commented weakly, clearly at a loss for words.

"You've made excellent progress!" Maggie congratulated her brightly, her voice brittle and forced.

"The blackmailer knew how much they could afford to pay?" DS Elliot asked thoughtfully.

"Yep. It's someone on the street. It has to be."

Heidi was still speaking in clipped, almost aggressive tones.

"Well... I'll admit it does seem most likely-" he began.

"The blackmailer knew how much each business could afford. The break-ins have only happened on this street. Kitty mentioned that she lost her keys for a few days. I'm thinking the blackmailer took them and made a copy. For that they need to be close and to look like they belong here. Which all adds up to it being someone from the street."

Heidi crossed her arms as she spoke, daring him to contradict her, but at Maggie's gasp she let her arms fall.

"What is it?" she asked quickly.

"Lost keys!" Maggie exclaimed, her hands going to her mouth.

They all looked at her enquiringly and she took a deep breath.

"I lost my keys too!"

"What?! When?!" Heidi demanded.

"Weeks ago," Maggie admitted.

"Weeks ago?! And you didn't say anything?! Even after the break-ins?!"

"Because I found them! They were only missing for a few hours and then I found them on the floor behind the desk! I thought they'd just fallen out of my bag, but now..."

She trailed off, wringing her hands unhappily.

Heidi's stomach twisted at the sight.

"It's fine, I would have thought the same," she told her, her voice softening ever so slightly.

"You think someone took Maggie's keys?!" Shelley

asked in obvious horror.

"And copied them," Heidi confirmed.

"You need to change the locks," DS Elliot told her firmly.

Heidi looked at the door, fumbling with her own thoughts.

"He's right. I know you don't make changes to the shop, as a rule, but this is different. This is your safety we're talking about. Your father would want you to," Maggie told her determinedly.

"Kitty is getting the locks changed at the florist. She's going to use the money she's not paying the blackmailer."

That made Maggie chuckle.

"Good for her! Not paying, is she? Very sensible. Things like that never end!"

I asked her to wait a day before changing them though," Heidi added.

"Really? Why?!"

"Because her next payment is meant to be tonight, and I'm going to catch the blackmailer in the act!"

Chapter 12

Heidi was not unfamiliar with the phenomenon of stopping conversations in their tracks, but the silence that met these words was pretty spectacular.

"I'm sorry, what?" DS Elliot managed eventually.

"I'm going to stake out the flower shop, and see who the blackmailer is."

It wasn't a particularly complicated sentence, but everyone seemed to struggle with it.

"The flower shop?" Maggie asked.

"The blackmailer?" Shelley queried.

"I don't understand," DS Elliot admitted.

"What's not to understand? I know where the blackmailer is going to be tonight, trying to collect money from Kitty, so I'm going to be there and catch them."

"But don't we think the blackmailer is the killer?" Maggie asked, nonplussed.

"Yes, we do. That's exactly the point!" Heidi confirmed, bordering on exasperation now.

"But what are you going to do?" Shelley asked as DS

Elliot began massaging the bridge of his nose and pacing quickly up and down.

"Well, I'll hide in the back room, or maybe at the bottom of the stairs up to Kitty's flat," Heidi suggested.

"And when the killer finds you?!" DS Elliot snapped.

"Well that's when she'll be murdered, obviously," Maggie told him calmly.

"No! I'll be out of sight, *obviously*!" Heidi explained, impatiently.

"Got an invisibility cloak, have you?!" he demanded.

"Well, no but-"

"When the killer arrives and there isn't any money waiting for them, do you really think they won't look around for it? That they won't find you?!"

Heidi felt an uncomfortable squirming in her chest and refrained from answering.

"Were you even going to call me to clue me in on this brilliant plan?!" he asked her.

"I might have..."

"This person is dangerous! Someone is already dead!" he reminded her.

"I know that! I found her body right there!" Heidi told him, pointing to the middle of the shop, her face flushed and her eyes bright.

"So why aren't you taking this seriously?!"

"I am! I am serious about finding out who did this!"

188

she replied hotly.

"I know that you knew her, but just because Lydia Wickes was your friend, doesn't mean you should-"

"She wasn't my friend, she was horrible, you're completely missing the point here!" Heidi cut in.

"What *is* the point?"

Heidi had absolutely no answer for this question prepared. She couldn't even begin to explain why she was so keen to apprehend Lydia's killer. She'd backed herself into a conversational blind alley and she had no idea where to go from there.

"Alright, so maybe I don't have all the *minutia* of details figured out yet, but I will have by this evening!" she told him.

"Are you joking?! This is the most ridiculously slap-dash plan I've ever heard! I doubt you're capable of planning anything!" he told her hotly.

At this, Maggie and Shelley could no longer remain spectators.

"Actually, she's a great planner," Shelley cut in quietly but sincerely.

"Very detail oriented!" Maggie agreed solemnly.

"Thank you!" Heidi told them, feeling vindicated.

"Oh really! Planned lots of stake-outs have you? Got a few police under-cover operations under your belt?" Heidi crossed her arms in obvious disdain of this ridiculous question and glared at DS Elliot for all she was worth.

"You're only leading this case because you were the closest police officer when it got called in!" she told him coldly, "well I was closer than you, so by that reasoning, I'd be the better person to handle it."

He flushed angrily, his eyes flashing, and Heidi knew she had hit a nerve. She'd meant to.

The trouble with consuming so much literature, and watching people with such analytical detachment, was that it made it terribly easy to script your own cutting remarks. Usually, Heidi didn't say them, she was content to think them and move on, but anger was surging through her every inch, and the words burst out before she could stop them.

Now however, she was filled with remorse. DS Elliot didn't respond. He didn't retaliate, or argue back. He didn't defend himself or argue his case. He just looked at her.

"I'm sure you're very good at your job," Heidi tacked on, her voice now small and apologetic.

Still, DS Elliot didn't speak.

"You wouldn't have been given the case otherwise," she ventured.

He still said nothing and Heidi was beginning to panic. She cast a desperate look at Maggie and Shelley, who both stepped forward quickly.

"Oh absolutely!" Maggie told him.

"Definitely!" Shelley agreed.

"We have every confidence in you!" Maggie assured him, her hands to her chest.

"I shouldn't have lost my temper," Heidi murmured, her eyes downcast.

DS Elliot frowned at them all, his expression unreadable.

"I think you might all be crazy," he said eventually.

Heidi looked affronted but Maggie nodded reasonably.

"Entirely possible. It takes a certain sort of person to work in a bookshop," she confessed.

"I would like to point out that I really have nothing to do with this whole thing. *I'm* not investigating or anything," Shelley reminded them.

"True. You have some sense of self preservation. But *you two*," he rounded on Maggie and Heidi, "you two are clearly mad and if you're not careful you're going to get yourselves killed."

Heidi muttered something about being a very careful person, but a sharp look from DS Elliot silenced her.

"There will be no hiding out waiting for killers," he declared.

"We can't waste this opportunity!" Heidi argued.

"It does seem providential that the potential

murderer is going to be *right there*," Maggie weedled.

"The key words there are 'potential murderer,'" DS Elliot responded flatly.

"So you're just going to let them get away?" Heidi asked, horrified.

"No, I will arrange for police to be there and apprehend the suspect," he told them.

Maggie looked mollified but Heidi pursed her lips in displeasure.

"What?" he asked her.

"You're going to go yourself and catch them?" she asked suspiciously.

"Yes, what's wrong with that?"

"What if you don't get approval before tonight? It's pretty short notice for a formal stake-out, isn't it?"

"I'll be there," he insisted.

"No matter what?"

"No matter what."

"What if your superior officer expressly forbids it?" she asked.

"Why on earth would they do that?" he queried.

"Because they don't want to follow the hunch of some random cursed bookseller," she suggested.

"You do know this isn't a book, right? In real life, the police follow up every lead and every clue and they pretty much never believe in curses."

Heidi was unconvinced but thought better of arguing further. Even she could admit, though not outloud of course, that she hadn't really had a plan, and in hindsight it probably would have been very hard to come up with one that wouldn't have resulted in her untimely death.

"I'll need to get back to the station and get the ball rolling," he told them, giving them a final anxious look before leaving.

"Well that was entertaining," Maggie commented happily, watching him go.

Heidi didn't say anything, she was still feeling a confusing jumble of emotions and didn't know how she wanted to react. Sensing her unease, Maggie turned to her with a guilty expression.

"I'm sorry, Heidi dear. He was asking about you and I suppose we just got carried away," she explained.

"We didn't mean to say anything we shouldn't, and we definitely didn't mean to say anything bad!" Shelley added.

Heidi nodded slowly, words still not coming.

"I never meant to imply that there's anything *wrong* with you," Maggie hurried on, "I hope that you didn't think I was, well, criticising."

"There isn't anything wrong with me," Heidi repeated, insistence in the words.

"Of course not!"

"Not everyone has to be sociable!" Heidi told them.

"No, no, absolutely!"

"Of course I was a chatty child, all children are chatty," Heidi snapped.

"Quite right!"

"It doesn't mean I'm- there's nothing that-"

Heidi faltered, not sure where to go from there.

"I'm fine," she finished after a moment.

"Of course!" Shelley agreed.

"If you say so, dear," Maggie offered.

Heidi turned to her with narrowed eyes but was met with a look of complete innocence.

"What's that supposed to mean?" Heidi demanded.

"Nothing, I'm sure you're very happy," Maggie told her.

"Yes," Heidi agreed after a pause, "Yes I am. I have a lovely life."

"It's nice to have the bookshop open again," Shelley chimed in brightly, obviously keen to turn the conversation.

"Yes, I wonder if we'll have any customers," Maggie replied.

"Surely *someone* will come in."

As it was, it was nearly three in the afternoon before they saw their first sign of life, and even that wasn't a paying customer.

"Open as usual are you?" Alexander Price asked in his booming voice.

"Not that you'd know it," Maggie replied gesturing to the empty space.

"Ah my dear lady, I'm sure things will pick up soon! This drought cannot last forever, our fortunes must change with time!"

"Slow at your shop too, is it?" Maggie asked him sympathetically.

"Alas, yes. Barely a soul all day, but no matter! As I say, the tides must turn eventually!"

"I saw Lizzie and Jane when I went for lunch. They're quiet too. Not as quiet as us, but they're still in a total panic. If things carry on like this they won't be able to afford their rent," Shelley told them all.

"Poor dears, I hope they'll be alright!" Maggie exclaimed.

"Maybe if the killer is caught, everything will calm down," Heidi suggested.

Maggie opened her mouth excitedly, clearly ready to tell Mr Price about the stake-out planned for that evening, but Heidi silenced her with a look.

"Have you seen Rose around?" Maggie asked instead, blushing slightly but covering the moment well.

"I have, the poor, dear girl seems to be holding up

well, though I did detect some trouble in paradise!" Mr Price told them in a stage whisper.

"Trouble in paradise?"

"Indeed, there was definite tension between the lovely Rose and her paramour."

"Rose and Robert are fighting?" Shelley translated.

"I wonder why!" Maggie exclaimed, looking surprised but excited.

Heidi knew what she was thinking. Had Rose discovered something about Robert? Did she suspect him of being involved in her mother's death? It would certainly cause tension if she did.

"Perhaps I'll go and buy us some cakes," Heidi suggested.

"A wonderful idea!" Maggie agreed.

"One for you, Mr Price?" Heidi offered.

"A charming offer, but sadly I must depart! Au revoir dear ladies!"

"At least he doesn't seem to be worried about his business," Shelley commented once he was gone.

"No, I think he does a lot of business online. He always has boxes and boxes, coming in and going out all the time," Maggie explained.

"How do you know that Maggie? When have you been spending time in Alexander's shop?" Shelley asked, arching one eyebrow, "Developed an interest in model airplanes, have you?"

"Never you mind about my interests young lady!" Maggie scolded playfully, "Heidi, I'll take the chocolatiest cake they have, please."

Heidi set off, determined to exude confidence and self assurance, to get Rose talking and convince her to open up. If Rose had real concerns about Robert, Heidi wanted to know about them. She approached the bakery with her head held high, ready to shut down any talk about curses and get straight to the point. As she reached the door, she paused, taking a deep breath. She'd just made to step inside when a sound caught her ear and stopped her in her tracks. Angry voices were coming from inside and Heidi was certain that one of them was Rose.

"Shouldn't you be at work?!" she was hissing.

"What's that supposed to mean?!" the other voice replied.

It was Robert. He sounded upset and angry and Heidi shifted a little closer, making sure she was completely concealed from view.

"You know what I mean! You should be at work! How can you afford to take all this time off?!" Rose demanded.

"I *asked* for time off, to be here to support you! You just lost your mum! I thought you'd want me around!"

The hurt he was feeling was evident in his voice but

Rose wasn't softening.

"I just think we need the money! It's not like you have any other income coming in, is it?" Rose probed.

"There will be some money from your mum though, won't there? And besides-" he rushed on, "you're more important than money!"

"I don't know about mum. I never really knew what she was thinking. I think most of what she had was in the business. It was doing really well, but I don't know what that would mean for money," Rose sighed, "I have no idea how any of this works. I wish my dad was here."

"Your dad?! When did you last see him?!" Robert snapped, clearly stung.

"Not since I was little, but- he's still my dad," Rose muttered.

"Well I could try to find him for you then," Robert suggested, clearly searching for some more positive footing.

"The police are looking for him. They think he must have changed his name. Mum always told me he was a soldier, but I think he must have been a bit... well, a bit of a rogue."

"A rogue?" Robert laughed, "that's a romantic way to put it."

"So?!" Rose snapped.

"Well- I just-"

"So what if I want to be romantic about it?! So what

if I want my dad?! What's wrong with that Robert?! What's your problem?!"

"I don't have a problem," he grumbled, sounding suddenly like a surly teenager.

"It seems like you do! You had a problem with my mum, you have a problem with my dad, maybe you have a problem with me!" she shouted.

"Rose! I love you! I don't have a problem with you at all! I'm sorry! I-"

"Just go back to work Robert," she snapped.

There was silence, and Heidi waited with bated breath to see what would happen next. She only just had time to jump back when she heard the soft clip of footsteps, before Robert burst out of the doorway and strode down the street. Heidi stepped forward immediately, not giving herself time to reconsider. She wanted to see Rose, to make sure that she was alright, and see her reaction to the argument, but she stopped at the sight of Rose's stricken face.

"He didn't do it- he wouldn't…" she muttered before bursting into tears.

Heidi didn't have much experience comforting people and it was becoming a disconcertingly regular occurrence at this point. She shuffled forward and reached out a hand to pat Rose on the shoulder. It felt insufficient but the counter was between them, limiting her options.

"I'm so sorry, you must think I'm ridiculous- always crying like this," Rose sniffed.

"You're grieving, I'm pretty sure crying is normal," Heidi pointed out.

Rose chuckled softly and held her apron up to her eyes.

"I don't think anything about all this is normal," she said.

"That's true. But I still don't think crying is unreasonable," Heidi shrugged.

Rose sighed and let the apron fall away from her swollen, red-rimmed eyes.

"I just wish it was all over. Or that it had never happened. I was happy, you know?"

Heidi did know. She understood this feeling perfectly, but even Rose didn't need her to point out that there was no going back.

"Fighting with Robert can't help," she commented instead.

Rose's expression darkened.

"You know that's your fault."

"My fault?!" Heidi exclaimed.

"Yes, yours! You planting ideas in my head! Robert would never hurt anyone! But you got me all turned around, thinking about mum not wanting us to get married, and always being on at him about money!"

"But that's all true, isn't it?"

"That doesn't mean he killed her! It doesn't make him a blackmailer either!" Rose snapped.

"Were you being blackmailed?" Heidi asked interestedly.

"No, nothing to be blackmailed *about*. You?"

"No, same here."

"I don't know what's happened to this street. It used to be a community! It used to feel safe!" Rose mourned.

"It is! Or- it will be. I still think maybe what happened to your mum and the blackmailing and break-ins is all connected. It's all just one awful thing, so when it's over, everything will go back to normal," Heidi told her, tripping over her words a little.

"It won't all go back to normal," Rose reminded her sadly.

"True. Sorry. That was a stupid thing to say, I just meant-" Heidi broke off, not sure how to go on.

"I know what you meant. I hope you're right."

"Do you really not know where your dad is?" Heidi asked, changing the subject.

"Nope. I haven't seen him since I was about three. I barely even remember him, just the tattoo on his shoulder of mum's name. I used to trace it with my finger. It's not much of a memory is it?"

"It's something. And maybe he'll come back. Maybe

201

the police will find him and tell him about your mum and he'll come to see you," Heidi suggested.

"If he does come back, I'm starting to think it would be just for money. That Mr Darcy said something about dad... and mum made a comment after that, that made me think he might not be the best person. Mum never wanted to talk about him, so I just sort of learned not to ask, but now I'm starting to hear things about him," Rose sighed deeply, running a hand through her hair in a distracted way.

"So your mum did know Mr Darcy before the party?" Heidi asked.

"I guess so, yeah. Seems like my dad did too, but I definitely don't get the impression that they were friends."

Heidi hummed thoughtfully to herself on the walk back to Cross-Town Books, as she filed her new information away. It felt like edge pieces of a jigsaw were beginning to fit together, but she still had no idea was the picture was of. There was only one option- she needed to gather more pieces.

"I think I'm going to go to the stake-out," she announced as she set down the box of cakes in front of Maggie.

Chapter 13

Heidi debated with herself for a long time before finally deciding on an outfit. It wasn't because she cared about the opinion of DS Elliot, obviously, she had no interest at all in impressing him, she just wasn't sure what would be the correct clothing for the situation. Clearly the all-black ensemble she had donned for the break-in at Luscious Whisper had been a mistake, but it didn't feel right to just dress normally either. Eventually she decided on a slightly mish-mashed outfit, consisting of a pair of her father's black jeans, generously rolled up at the ankle, and a dark blue top of her mother's. She couldn't be accused of dressing like a cat-burglar this time, but she also wouldn't draw attention to herself out in the dark. With a last nod to herself in the mirror, she turned to go.

"Are you sure about this?" her mother's voice called her back.

"Of course she is! This is her plan! She deserves to see it through," her father cut in excitedly.

Joan gave a grunt, making her presence known but

not hazarding an opinion.

"It'll be fine, DS Elliot will be there," Heidi told her mother.

"Yes..." Alice sighed, still looking uncertain.

"She's going to solve a mystery!" Phillip told his wife, practically bouncing on his toes.

"I am. I'm going to solve a mystery. I'm going to find out who killed Lydia- who's been blackmailing people and stealing from all of us."

With that, Heidi squared her shoulders and left, running down the stairs and out into the night, leaving her ghosts behind her. She made her way to the next street and walked back down it as casually as possible, until she reached the back entrance to the flower shop. She knocked gently, just as she had agreed to do, and the door was immediately opened by a pale faced Kitty.

"Are you sure about this?" she asked quietly.

"Of course!" Heidi replied, studying the woman closely.

She looked clear eyed, but tired, and Heidi suspected that her newfound sobriety was taking a toll.

"You OK?" she asked evenly, hesitant to press the matter.

"I'm fine, just..." Kitty trailed off, massaging one temple, "your policeman isn't here yet."

"He's not *my* policeman, and I'm glad he's not here

yet, he'd only make a fuss and try to get me to leave."

"But you don't want to leave."

"No I do not. This was my plan," Heidi retorted.

Kitty smiled at that but shook her head.

"You might be crazy," she said.

"You have no idea," Heidi sighed.

Kitty gave her a questioning look but Heidi pressed on.

"I'm going to get situated. Don't mention I'm here when you let him in, alright? Just open the door for him and then get back upstairs where it's safe. And lock your door."

Kitty nodded and ushered Heidi through to the shop before leaving her, in the semi-darkness of the closed business. If there was a chance that anyone was watching, then Heidi didn't want to alert them to her presence, so she navigated by the limited light coming in through the windows. She opted for the corner by the work-bench and settled herself in to wait. She had a partial view of the shop and she should be able to lean forward to see more once she heard the shop door open. She'd just started wishing that she'd brought a book or maybe some snacks, when she heard DS Elliot arrive. It had to be DS Elliot and whatever police forces he'd been able to muster, because it was over an hour too early for the blackmailer and she assumed that the blackmailer would be coming in through the shop, since all the activity had been on Cross Street.

"What are you doing here?" he demanded upon seeing her.

This didn't seem to Heidi to be a particularly auspicious start, so she casually ignored him and awaited a more receptive greeting.

"Miss Cross! Why are you here?!" he demanded again, stepping towards her.

She lifted her eyes to his and fixed him with a glare.

"To catch a killer."

"That's *my* job!" he reminded her hotly.

"And you're going to do it by standing around, shouting and scaring them off? Excellent plan," she commented with a sickly smile.

He stepped towards her, out of view of the doorway, and dropped his voice to a hiss.

"No, I'm going to do it by waiting here, quietly and apprehending the culprit when they enter!"

"Yes, that was my plan, if you recall," she reminded him.

"Yes," he sighed, "but you're not a police officer! You're not trained to stop a killer!" he shot back.

"So I'll leave the apprehending bit to you then, but I want to see who it is!" she insisted.

"Why?!"

"They stole my bell."

It appeared that DS Elliot had no response for this. He stared at her for a moment in indecision and then dropped down onto the floor beside her with a huff. They sat there in silence, neither of them sure what to say next, until finally Heidi piped up.

"Where's your backup?"

"You were right, we couldn't put together a team at such short notice. Not without more to go on, anyway," he admitted.

"Your boss doesn't think the blackmail and the murder are related?" she asked.

"He's not convinced one way or the other. I think he quite likes the idea that Lydia Wickes was murdered because everyone is desperate to date Charles Bingley, to be honest."

Heidi scrunched up her nose.

"Doesn't that seem a bit silly?"

"People are silly sometimes. Still, I think it is more likely that she surprised a blackmailing thief and died because of it," he agreed.

"So you're doing the stake-out on your own?"

"Apparently not," he pointed out, nudging her shoulder with his.

"I suppose you're lucky I'm here then!"

He wasn't prepared to go so far as admitting to this, and instead changed the conversation quickly.

"You're name is Cross and the street is Cross Street," he said, "is there a connection, or-?"

"Just a coincidence really, though it was the fact that tipped the scales and convinced dad to take the plunge. He always wanted to run a bookshop, it was his dream, so when premises became available on Cross Street, he thought it was a sign. We bought it right away and moved in!"

He watched her closely as she spoke, his gaze making her skin prickle.

"And so Cross-Town Books was born," he said, turning away as though he could sense her discomfort.

"Exactly. It was literally a dream come true! Mum and dad ran the shop and I played there every day after school, and we all lived upstairs, and mum made the flat so beautiful-"

She stopped abruptly when she caught herself running on.

"It sounds wonderful! So you always wanted to run the shop?" he asked.

"No, not really, I mean-"

Again she stopped, hating that she couldn't seem to complete a normal sentence when talking to this man. He was asking these questions as though they were normal chit-chat and not huge, world-shaping truths.

"No?"

"No. I love the shop. I completely love the shop. I love running it. I love working there. But, when I was little I didn't think about running the shop because that was what my mum and dad did, and I didn't know I would lose them," she explained.

"What happened?" he asked gently.

"A car accident when I was eight. I barely remember it, I'm not sure why. My aunt Joan was round, looking after me while mum and dad were out, and they just didn't come home. The next day police came to talk to us, but Joan made me stay in my room. I don't know any of the details."

"You didn't ask later?"

"Joan didn't want to talk about it. She wasn't much of a talker at the best of times, and losing my dad broke her heart. She was his aunt really, and we were all the family she had. She adored my dad, so it was all just too painful. She left her whole life behind and moved in with me to raise me and keep the shop going for my parents."

"She sounds like a lovely woman," he said softly.

Heidi didn't reply. The word 'lovely' didn't quite fit Joan somehow. She was selfless. She was dignified. She was intelligent, but she wasn't lovely. *Lovely* great aunts wore fluffy pink cardigans and carried sweets with them, they didn't keep bookshops running and teach their great nieces about classic literature. They didn't advise against parties and play-dates, and council against relationships. Joan had been wonderful in her own way, but she had definitely been unique.

"Did you always know you wanted to do this?" Heidi asked.

"What, a stake-out?"

"Be police," Heidi corrected, rolling her eyes.

"Ah! That! Yeah, I did really. Ever since I was a kid I wanted to be in law enforcement. I started out wanting to be batman of course, but over time I settled for commissioner Gordon." DS Elliot told her.

Heidi blinked at him, uncomprehending.

"Commissioner Gordon? The policeman from batman?" he tried again.

"Sorry," Heidi shrugged.

"You'd have been more comfortable with a more literary reference, huh?"

"It's what I was raised on," she agreed.

"I'm ashamed to say, I was never much of a reader," he confessed.

"Never much of a reader?" Heidi repeated the words as though she couldn't quite understand them.

"I just never really saw the appeal, when TV and films are so much quicker."

"Since when is quicker better?!" Heidi demanded.

"You know what I mean, its more convenient to put

a film on, and you can even do something else while you watch."

"That's exactly why books are better! Don't get me wrong, I love TV and films too, but books are like magic! You get to really step into another world! Not just lend it half an ear while you're cleaning or working out or something, but really, fully, immerse yourself in it!"

Her voice had risen as she spoke and she flushed, pressing a hand to her mouth.

"Sorry, I've never been on a stake-out before, I'm not great at keeping quiet," she whispered.

"I think that's the loudest I've heard you!" he chuckled under his breath.

She checked the time quickly, hoping that she hadn't risked being overheard at all. It was almost twelve, the blackmailer could be arriving any minute. DS Elliot checked his own watch and they both quietened down, watching the darkness of the shop through the open archway. The longer Heidi looked, the more she could make out- the shelves of succulents, the potted flowers on the counter, the displays against the far wall. The gentle hum of the walk-in fridge and their own breathing was the only sound to be detected. The door didn't creak open, a key didn't turn in the lock, nothing. The silence dragged on, making Heidi's skin itch. Her legs grew stiff now that they were all she had to think about. A sharp pain cut from her hip to her knee, from her unusual position sat on the floor. She checked her phone again after what felt like hours, and was amazed to see that it was only twenty past midnight. No sign of the blackmailer yet. She could feel DS Elliot's discomfort too, as he tried to stretch out his legs as slowly and quietly as possible. He checked the time next, and Heidi leaned over to see the display. Twelve forty-five.

Where was the blackmailer?!

By one in the morning, Heidi had stopped feeling her sore legs. Her extremities all felt numb and she was starting to zone out. The next thing she really knew, DS Elliot was gently touching one arm and whispering her name.

"What?!" she gasped, sitting up suddenly.

"You were dozing off a bit," he told her with a smile.

"Dozing off? Where?" she mumbled, still coming back to herself.

"We're still in the flower shop, but no one showed."

"No one showed?"

"Nope."

"No one showed?!" she said again, massaging her legs furiously.

"I guess not, it's gone two now."

"But we did a stake-out! How could they not show?!" she demanded, feeling tired, vulnerable and affronted.

"Well to be fair, they didn't *know* we were going to do a stake-out," he pointed out reasonably.

"No! They thought there would be money waiting for them! So why on earth didn't they show up?!" Heidi asked, clearly still offended that her plan had come to nothing.

"Maybe they had a change of plan? Maybe killing Lydia Wickes changed things? Perhaps they thought it would be too risky," he suggested.

"Coward! If you're going to blackmail people, you should at least show up to collect your ill-gotten-gains and get caught!" Heidi fumed.

She knew that she wasn't being reasonable, but she'd been very proud of her plan, and waking from an impromptu sleep to find DS Elliot so very close had done nothing to improve her feelings on the situation.

"Ill-gotten-gains?" DS Elliot repeated with a laugh.

"What would you call it? Loot?" she snapped.

"Maybe if I was a character in an Agatha Christie novel I would," he told her with a broad smile.

"A literary reference? You're improving."

"Or just trying to impress you."

She flushed but didn't reply. She felt as though she were spending half her life at the moment with her face suffused with colour.

"So what do we do now? This was my only plan!" she

grumbled.

"Luckily I have a few more avenues under investigation," he crowed.

"Does that mean you've found Lydia's ex-husband?" she asked quickly.

His face fell.

"Or worked out how she knew Mr Darcy?" she added.

"Wait, what?"

"Or maybe you've found some of the stolen items?" she suggested.

"Ah! Maybe!" he cut in triumphantly.

"You have?!"

"Well, it's just a possibility at the moment, we're still working to verify it. A couple of items matching the right description have turned up at a second-hand shop across town with a bit of a dicey reputation. We don't know for sure though! I shouldn't really have mentioned it at all, I just..."

he trailed off, embarrassed, and Heidi couldn't help but smile.

"I think I'll follow up with Mr Darcy then, if I can," Heidi told him brightly.

"Mr Darcy? The other owner of the gin shop? Who all the women are falling over themselves for?" he asked in an expressionless voice.

"That's the one, though Mr Bingley is the favourite. But Mr Darcy knew Lydia years ago and I want to know how."

Heidi had expected an argument, but none materialised. She heaved herself to her feet and flexed her ankles to try to bring blood back into her limbs, and DS Elliot was still looking thoughtful and distracted.

"Everything alright?" Heidi asked him.

"Yes! Yes of course, this has been nice," he told her with a vague smile before pulling himself up, his eyes clearing, "Sorry, I mean, it was a good stake-out, though no one came."

"Definitely the best stake-out I've ever been on," Heidi agreed.

"You said you didn't always want to work in the bookshop," he said suddenly, catching her off guard.

"Not when I was little, no," she agreed in surprise.

"What did you want to do then?"

"I wanted to be a detective," she admitted, her chin held defiantly high.

That same broad, dimple-inducing grin stretched back across his face.

Chapter 14

"Heidi!" Maggie cried delightedly from behind the counter, as she staggered into the shop the following morning.

Heidi cringed slightly at the sound. Her head felt tender after a night without much sleep. Even after she'd got home from the flower shop, she'd struggled to settle. Her back ached from the hours spent propped up against the wall waiting for someone who never showed, and her thoughts had run on a loop until she finally dozed off around dawn.

"Morning Maggie," she managed, massaging one temple.

"Oh dear, paying for your success, are you?"

"Paying for what?" Heidi asked, confused.

"Come on, come on, I want all the details! What exactly happened last night?!" Maggie demanded.

"There's not much to tell."

"How can you say that?! I want a full play by play! Who was it?! How did you do it?! Are they under arrest?!"

Maggie fired off.

"No, of course they're not, they never showed up," Heidi told her, wishing that Maggie would lower her voice a little.

"What?"

"They didn't show up," Heidi repeated.

"But I don't understand. If they didn't show up, how did you get it back?" Maggie asked her.

"Get *what* back?" Heidi asked helplessly.

"The bell!"

Maggie pointed as she spoke and Heidi's legs carried her forward unbidden. She followed Maggie's gaze and there it was, back on the desk exactly where it should be, her father's bell.

"It's back," she muttered faintly.

"You didn't get it back?" Maggie asked, the reality sinking in.

"No! We waited and waited but the blackmailer never showed up! We thought they had decided it was just too risky after killing Lydia..."

"They must have had a change of heart," Maggie suggested uncertainly.

Heidi could see that Maggie wasn't convinced by this notion, even as she said the words. What thief and blackmailer returns stolen goods? Why take the risk?

All morning, Heidi's eyes kept being drawn back to

the bell. She could barely form a coherent thought and she was grateful that the shop was so quiet. The bell's return just made no sense- why would the killer give it back?

Elizabeth stopped in at lunch time and made an immediate beeline for Heidi.

"Did you do it?!" she asked in a fierce whisper. Her eyes were bright and her cheeks were flushed.

"Sorry?"

"Did you catch them?" Elizabeth explained, "you must have done something! Some cash was left in the shop last night and a bracelet that had been taken was returned! Is it over?"

"Our bell was returned last night too," Heidi told her, not sure how to answer the question.

"Your bell?"

"My dad's old shop bell was taken. I always kept it behind the desk but it was stolen a few days ago," Heidi explained, marvelling at the fact that it really had only been a few days. It was starting to feel like years.

"They took your dad's bell?! That's so... spiteful!"

Heidi shrugged.

"At least it's back," she offered.

"But we still don't know who it was? Was it really the same person who killed Lydia?" Elizabeth asked.

"I have no idea. I was pretty sure that it was, but now..." Heidi trailed off, not sure how to put her thoughts

218

into words.

Mr Price stopped in to visit with Maggie in the afternoon, and they filled him in on the bell's return.

"Really?! So our thief is attempting to change their spots are they?! Is this remorse for killing Lydia I wonder?" Mr Price pondered.

"It must be, mustn't it?" Shelley asked delightedly.

"What else could it be?" Heidi mused aloud.

"Perhaps I should leave my door unlocked tonight, and see if some of my things return!" Mr Price suggested with a chuckle.

"What was taken from you?" Heidi asked, curious, just as Maggie asked why he would need to leave his door unlocked.

"The thief doesn't seem to need doors to be left unlocked," she reminded him.

"I took the precaution of changing the locks after the last night-time visitation. I recommend that you do the same, even if the thief has had a change of heart. You know what they say about leopards, after all!"

He swept out of the shop in his usual theatrical manner, after placing a kiss gingerly on Maggie's hand.

"Things seem to be going well there," Shelley commented with a grin.

"Oh we'll see," Maggie murmured vaguely.

"What, you're not keen?" Shelley pressed.

"He's a little young for me," Maggie replied, blushing.

"How young is he?" Heidi asked.

"At least ten years younger than me," Maggie admitted.

"And how old are you?"

"Never you mind that, young lady! I am young at heart!" Maggie snapped.

"Well then, there's no problem is there!" Shelley told her, laughing.

"Hmmmm," Maggie grumbled, but refused to commit herself one way or the other.

The funeral was arranged for the following day, and despite Lydia's character in life, it seemed as though everyone on the street was planning to attend.

"Are you sure we should be going to this?" Heidi asked Maggie and Shelley for the tenth time, tugging at the sleeve of her black dress.

"Of course! It would be so rude not to!" Shelley told her again.

"Besides, DS Elliot is likely to be there," Maggie added.

"So? What does that have to do with anything?" Heidi demanded.

"It means that there's an opportunity to investigate of course! We can look out for anyone acting unusually! And DS Elliot can see you in that dress," Maggie told her, muttering the final remark under her breath.

"I suppose so," Heidi grumbled, "but funerals are..."

She didn't need to finish the thought, Maggie already understood. Funerals were an odd thing, in some ways they got more difficult the more you attended.

"We'll all go together, and we'll stick together. Alexander is going to walk over there with us too," Maggie told her reassuringly.

They were closing the shop for the afternoon so that they could attend the service and the reception, to be held, of all places, in Luscious Whisper. Apparently Lydia had left instructions in her will of how she wanted her funeral to be arranged, and between them Mary and Rose had put it together.

Heidi had been dreading it all morning, and the closer it drew, the more anxious she had become.

"Are you really sure we have to-" she began again, but Maggie cut her off.

"What do you think we should be looking for when we get there?" she asked abruptly.

"Sorry?"

"When we get to the funeral, should we be looking for people who are crying too much? Not crying at all? Or should we just be listening to conversations, seeing if we can pick up anything useful? How are we going to handle this investigation?" Maggie asked.

Right. This wasn't just a funeral, it was an investigation.

"I think we look for all of the above," Heidi told her thoughtfully, "And we look for anyone we don't know. Perhaps Lydia's ex-husband will come, we definitely need to talk to him."

"Rose's father? You think he'll be there?" Shelley asked.

"Well the police have been looking for him, to let him know about Lydia. If he's heard that she... passed away, then surely he'll come to the funeral?" Heidi theorised.

"That would be nice for Rose!" Shelley exclaimed happily.

Heidi wasn't so sure, but she didn't voice this. Rose was still clearly upset with Heidi for voicing her concerns about Robert. She needed to tread carefully where the mysterious father was concerned.

The bookshop was still so quiet that when there was thirty minutes left, they started the process of cleaning and locking up the shop. Through the windows, Heidi could see their neighbours doing the same, securing their shops and emerging onto the street, all dressed in sombre black.

"Alright, let's go."

They trailed outside, nodding to their friends as they made their way down the street to the church. It was small but beautiful, with the original stained glass and uncomfortable pews. Joan's funeral had been held here too, and Heidi's parents' years before that.

"I hate this place," she muttered as they approached.

"That's because you don't come here enough," Maggie told her.

"What?! I think I've been plenty actually," Heidi snapped back.

"You've only been for funerals! Of course you don't like it here! You should come for the church fête in the summer. And the Christmas service when all the children dress up. Mix in some good memories with the bad ones."

It wasn't a terrible suggestion, but Heidi just wrapped her arms around her middle and followed Maggie inside.

Rose was waiting with the vicar on one side and Robert on the other. He didn't look entirely comfortable but Heidi was pleased to see that he was there. Quite apart from wanting to keep an eye on him for the investigation, Heidi was hoping that if he turned out to be innocent, Rose and he might actually make it work as a couple. She didn't like the idea that her suspicions might cause them to break up when they'd been so happy.

"Thank you for coming," Rose told them a little stiffly when they reached her.

"Of course dear! We're so sorry for your loss!" Maggie told her, pulling her in for a hug.

It struck Heidi that this was actually a very fitting and diplomatic thing to say. Lydia's death was of course shocking and awful, but not too many people were really truly sad that she wasn't around any more. They were however, all very sorry that Rose had lost her mother.

"We're sorry for your loss," Heidi told Rose, her voice shaking a little, to her dismay.

Rose's eyes searched her face but Heidi wasn't sure what she was looking for, so she just held out a hand, which Rose slowly shook.

"Have you heard from your dad at all?" Shelley whispered, after giving Rose a hug and offering her own condolences.

Heidi immediately slowed her steps to listen to the reply.

"No, no one has been able to reach him. It seems like no one knows where he is! No one has seen him in years! I'm trying to find out more about him in general, in the hope it'll give me a place to start looking," Rose told her forlornly.

"Apparently he grew up in Derbyshire," Robert

added, "I've been calling round people and searching on social media. I'm sure we'll find him soon."

Rose gave him a small sad smile and slipped a hand into his, looking at Heidi almost defiantly.

She turned quickly away and moved further into the church, following the crowd of mourners as they chatted just a little too brightly.

"It doesn't quite have a funeral feel, does it?" Maggie commented in an undertone.

"Well... I suppose it's not quite... but then, lots of people prefer to see a funeral as a celebration of life!" Shelley attempted valiantly.

"Quite right dear," Maggie replied with a smirk.

Heidi refrained from comment, but she couldn't help agreeing with Maggie. People seemed to be treating the funeral as a social excursion, rather than an expression of collective grief and respect. They were chatting amongst themselves and there was a distinctly salacious feel to the proceedings, no doubt due to Lydia's remarkable cause of death. The atmosphere did dim slightly when the service began in earnest, but it never attained the sombre tones that a funeral demands. Things only got worse once the service was over and everyone trailed back up the road to Luscious Whisper for the wake.

"This is ridiculous," Maggie grumbled as they entered.

"It's what Lydia wanted," Shelley retorted uncertainly.

"Why?! I think she just wanted to make everyone uncomfortable," Maggie snapped.

It was certainly working so far. The shelves had all been pushed back as much as possible, but lace bras and even a rack of feather boas was still clearly visible. Rose and Mary had obviously done their best to disguise their surroundings with flower arrangements, but they ended up adding to the mish-mash of colours and the whole effect was almost overpowering.

"This place looks different in the daylight, doesn't it," Shelley commented diplomatically.

"Yes, the low lighting was definitely a sensible choice for the party! In the light of day it all seems terribly tawdry," Maggie exclaimed, gazing around them.

"I know," a voice lamented from behind them. They all turned and were horrified to find Rose.

"Oh, Rose dear!"

"It's alright Maggie, I know exactly what you mean. This place might be the perfect event space for bachelorette parties, but it's not right for a wake! Mum left specific instructions though, and we wanted to respect them," Rose explained.

"You and Mary? How are things going in that department?" Maggie asked quietly.

"I'm not really sure," Rose sighed, "the will hasn't formally been read yet, but I did find a copy in mum's safe in her flat."

Her lips were pursed and Heidi noticed that she looked decidedly unhappy.

"Did she not leave you the shop?! We were told she had!" Heidi exclaimed, bending the truth a little.

DS Elliot hadn't told them anything of the kind, at least not intentionally, but Heidi had been sure that she'd read him correctly.

"No, she did, I just found- I found the will, and read it on my own, but I wish she'd done things differently. She always promised the shop to Mary! She's been working for almost nothing for years and years! She's done everything for mum! I want to talk to her about it, but I'm not sure what to say, and every time I try, she just runs off!"

Maggie patted her arm consolingly.

"She's just upset. She's had a nasty shock. Give her some time to calm down and then you two can have a proper chat about it. Just be sure that you know what you want to say when you do. It's good of her to have helped you with the funeral after everything that's happened!" Maggie noted.

"And Robert too! He's been amazing! He was up at five this morning, shifting stuff around in here to make room for the buffet table!" Rose told them, glowing as she spoke.

"He's one of the good ones," Shelley told Rose with a smile.

"Yes. Yes he is," Rose agreed, giving another defiant look to Heidi. She even squared her shoulders as though preparing to fight for Robert's honour.

"Lovely!" Heidi responded weakly, earning herself a slight softening from Rose.

"You've all done a brilliant job!" Maggie announced, gesturing to their surroundings, "considering."

"We did our best. Mum selected the music, the venue, the flowers, the food, everything! We didn't really have to make any decisions, we just had to put it into effect. It cost a fortune, but that money comes out of the estate, and I was happy to pay Kitty for the flowers anyway."

Heidi noted that Rose was chewing her lip uncomfortably, no doubt thinking of Lydia's very public remarks about Kitty's drinking.

"She's a great florist, the flowers look beautiful. Orchids are an unusual choice," Shelley commented, admiring the nearest arrangement.

"They were mum's favourite flower," Rose explained.

"Not roses?!" Maggie asked, surprised.

"No, it was one of her favourite jokes actually. She always said roses were pedestrian. Not her favourite," Rose quoted unhappily, beginning to worry and pull at the order of service still clasped in her hands.

"How unkind," Maggie commented bluntly.

"She loved you though!" Shelley leapt in, unable to help herself.

"I know she did, in her way," Rose agreed, not looking at all comforted by the thought.

I think mum just fell into a life that she didn't want," she explained, "she was always boy mad apparently, and she ran off with dad when she was so young! He turned out not to be what she expected, but by then it was too late. She was always her mum's favourite, and she was spoiled. Life with my dad, never having enough money, I think it made her bitter and she never really lost that."

"But she built a successful business! She made all the money she could want, surely!" Shelley suggested.

"She did build the business, but she still always wanted what other people had- or at least, she didn't want *them* to have it. I don't know why."

Rose sounded so forlorn, that Heidi couldn't help it. She reached out and pulled her into a hug. It was awkward, but nice, and Rose seemed to appreciate the gesture. Maggie looked absolutely stunned!

"People are complicated," Heidi murmured when she pulled away.

"Well said dear," Maggie agreed, still looking shell-shocked.

"Is that Mr Bingley?" Rose asked, looking over Heidi's shoulder.

They all turned and waved as Mr Bingley entered, with Jane on his arm. They looked more as though they were attending a party than a funeral. Although they weren't behaving inappropriately, they both just seemed to glow.

"Things definitely look as though they're going well there!" Maggie commented, happily.

"I wonder if Mr Darcy is here," Heidi murmured, almost to herself.

"Mr Darcy?! I wouldn't have thought that he was *your* type!" Shelley told her, clearly a little horrified by the thought.

"No! I want to know how he knew Lydia!" Heidi explained briefly, before moving away to accost Jane and Charles.

They confirmed that Mr Darcy was around somewhere, and Heidi started weaving through the crowd, looking for his tall, dark form.

"Heidi!" Elizabeth breathed a small sigh of relief as she caught Heidi's arm.

"Elizabeth! Are you alright?"

The young woman looked exhausted. Her curls were wild and her eyes held an expression bordering on panic.

"Have you found anything out about the blackmailer?! Our deadline is approaching!" she asked quickly.

Heidi wasn't sure what to say. She had hoped to identify the blackmailer before Elizabeth and Jane had to pay any more money that they obviously couldn't spare, but she'd been disappointed.

"I don't think you should pay," she told Elizabeth after a moment's pause.

"What?!"

"What I mean is, some of the things the blackmailer took are actually being returned! And they never showed up to collect their last payment from Kitty! I waited there for hours, but the blackmailer never arrived! And she decided not to hide her secret anyway. I think that's really the best option," Heidi counselled her.

Elizabeth eyed Heidi with surprise and curiosity, distracted for the moment from her own troubles.

"Drinking," Heidi murmured quietly, "but she's stopped."

"Really?! I had no idea! Well good for her, sorting it out, but it's not the same! I could end up in prison!" Elizabeth hissed.

"What?! What did you do?!" Heidi exclaimed.

"Nothing!"

"Then how could you end up in prison?!" Heidi

demanded.

"I can't tell you!"

"If you didn't do anything wrong-" Heidi began, but Elizabeth cut her off.

"But I can't *prove* that I didn't do anything wrong! I have no idea, what's even going on but there's no way the police would believe that! Especially now!"

Heidi sighed, feeling drained.

"You're going to have to at least tell me *something*," she implored.

Elizabeth looked around anxiously and then dropped her voice incredibly low.

"Drugs!" she breathed.

"What?!"

"Shhh! But they're not mine! Not ours! I don't know where they came from!" Elizabeth explained, still in a whisper.

"I don't understand," Heidi told her desperately.

"Neither do I! They were sent to the shop! In the post! A big bag of the stuff!"

"You mean they were sent to the shop by mistake?" Heidi pressed.

"But they have our address on! Number 6, Cross Street, Cambridge. So how can I claim that it was a mistake?! I didn't know what to do so I locked them away in the back room. Then the blackmailer must have found them! And now someone has been murdered! I can't exactly go to the police with a big bag of drugs, with our address on, and expect them to believe that I'm innocent, can I!"

She'd whispered all of this information so quickly that Heidi took a moment to catch up. It was having trouble sinking in. It just didn't make any sense!

"But why would someone send you drugs?" she asked hopelessly.

"No one would!" Elizabeth snapped.

"Except that clearly someone did," Heidi pointed out.

"Well I don't know why! Or who!" Elizabeth insisted, burying her face in her hands, "Why did the blackmailer have to find them?!"

"Because they wanted to. Because they're awful! Because they sneak into our businesses and take things and poke around!" Heidi replied, her temper rising.

"I thought that this was a nice street," Elizabeth told her mournfully.

Heidi couldn't help agreeing. It seemed that there was an awful lot more going on under the surface of Cross Street than she had ever suspected.

Drugs? Blackmail? Murder? What on earth was happening here, and what was going to happen next?!

Chapter 15

Heidi eventually tracked Mr Darcy down, but he was already shrugging into his perfectly cut coat.

"Mr Darcy!" she called, making him turn.

The stare with which he fixed her caused her to blush to the roots of her hair and stammer incoherently.

"I-I-I'm I'm sorry! I just- I just need a word with you."

"Just the one? Good. I want to get out of here as soon as possible," he snapped.

"It was good of you to come!" Heidi told him, trying not to drive him from the building any quicker.

"It was polite," he explained, as one explaining manners to a chimp.

"And you knew Lydia, didn't you?" she pressed.

"Ms *Wickes*? Yes, I suppose you could say that."

"Why do you say it like that?" she demanded.

"I knew her under another name."

"Her maiden name?" Heidi asked.

"No, her maiden name was something else, began

with a 'B' if I remember correctly. I knew her under the name of Wickham. I was better acquainted with her husband," he explained, his face twisting into a sneer.

"Wickham?! Why was she going by Wickes then?! And why didn't she want anyone to know that she knew you?"

"Perhaps because she was a ridiculous creature, and her husband was a criminal. They set no store by morality, either of them," he told her.

"Do you know where her husband is now?" Heidi asked.

"No. Thank god, I don't. I knew him all my childhood, and that was more than enough. If I never see him again, I'll be a happy man."

Heidi almost laughed at this. She couldn't help it! It was just that Mr Darcy looked as though he'd never been happy in his life! If he smiled she thought his face might crack. Something of this must have shown in her expression, because Mr Darcy seemed to draw himself up even higher and glared down at her with obvious disdain.

"It'll be a relief to be out of here and away from this place!" he snapped, "what Charles was thinking, opening a business here, I can't imagine!"

Heidi was powerless in the face of such blatant hostility. She froze like a deer in the headlights, but thankfully Elizabeth came to her rescue, stepping forward and addressing Mr Darcy calmly.

"By all means, don't let us keep you. I'm sure you must have social engagements to attend? Affectionate friends, eagerly awaiting your arrival? With such pleasant manners, I'm sure you must!"

There was silence as they all waited for his cutting retort, but it never came. Instead a slight smile seemed to light his eyes as he regarded Elizabeth, standing before him with her head held high.

For some reason he thought better of leaving the wake at that precise moment, and instead stayed another hour, frowning around at everyone and criticising the food.

Heidi felt exhausted. She made her way back to Maggie and Shelley, both of whom looked at her sympathetically.

"Shall we go?" Maggie asked.

"Is that allowed?" Heidi checked anxiously.

"Of course it is dear. We've spoken to Rose, we've given our condolences, and I suspect that if there was going to be a dramatic scene identifying the killer, it would have happened by now," she assured her.

"Alright, let's go."

They said goodbye to Rose briefly, but they couldn't find Mary anywhere and they quickly gave up looking.

"Alexander never showed up," Maggie grumbled as they made their way back across the street to the bookshop.

"What?!" Heidi exclaimed.

"Oh don't get excited, he didn't really want to go in the first place, he only agreed to for me," Maggie explained, blushing furiously. This was so unlike bold and unflappable Maggie that Heidi didn't press the matter.

"The butcher from down on the corner didn't come either. Nor anyone from the practice at number twenty eight," Shelley told them.

Heidi tried to think this through. Was it more guilty to not attend the funeral? Or less? Her thoughts were like treacle.

"No DS Elliot either," Maggie commented sadly.

Just the mention of him made Heidi's stomach feel suddenly unsettled. Not butterflies exactly, but maybe ladybirds, or something else small and non-threatening.

"Maybe he knew nothing important to the case would happen," she suggested, a little stupidly.

"But you did talk to some people, did you find anything out? Anything we should relay to DS Elliot perhaps?" Maggie asked hopefully.

"Did I hear my name mentioned?"

He was leaning against the doorway to the bookshop, watching them approach. Maggie looked delighted, but Heidi froze mid-step.

Alright, maybe something a little bigger than ladybirds.

"I was just wondering if Heidi had gleaned any useful information at the funeral," Maggie told him.

They all turned to look at her so she delved into her bag and felt around for her keys, using the act of unlocking the door to buy herself a few seconds grace.

"I doubt I have anything useful, but I suppose we could all go to the reading corner and have an update session?" she suggested, holding the door wide and fixing DS Elliot with a look that she hoped communicated that he better be sharing information too.

The reading corner was actually for children, but it was the only place in the shop with enough seats for all of them. Maggie, claiming seniority, took the big armchair. Heidi and Shelley, with the advantage of being familiar with the setup, hurried and grabbed the padded bench. This left DS Elliot cringing as he settled himself onto a beanbag chair that rustled and sighed beneath him.

Heidi smiled to herself as she watched him attempt to look in the least bit dignified, a feat that was entirely impossible when beanbags were involved.

"Alright, what did you find out at the funeral?" he demanded, once he'd given up on finding a better position.

"Why weren't you there yourself?" Maggie countered.

"I didn't want to put people off talking. If they knew

a police officer was there, people would have been on guard. I sent an officer in plain clothes instead, to gather information quietly," he told them.

"A spy?! At a funeral?!" Shelley exclaimed, horrified.

"The funeral of a murder victim dear. Do be sensible," Maggie told her soothingly.

"So what did your officer find out?" Heidi asked.

"I don't know yet, I'll find out tomorrow. I thought I would speak to you first, you know most of the people who attended," he told her.

"Well we didn't know everyone," Heidi admitted.

"But everyone in the street," Maggie cut in.

"Which is our suspect pool," Heidi added.

"*Why* is that our suspect pool?" Shelley asked imploringly.

"Because, our suspect is the thief! They knew how much money to blackmail Elizabeth and Jane for! They were able to sneak around borrowing keys without being noticed as out of place! They were-" Maggie started rattling off.

"Alright! Alright! Our suspect pool is the street," Shelley agreed unhappily.

"So did anyone say anything?" DS Elliot pressed.

"Well lots of people actually didn't go. Lydia really wasn't very well liked," Heidi told him.

"What about Mr Bingley? I would have thought he

would have been enough to draw a crowd," DS Elliot commented wryly.

"Oh well all the *ladies* attended, of course!" Maggie confirmed.

"But not the butcher, or anyone from the leather-work store!" Shelley told him.

"Or the man who runs the post office, or even Mr Price," Heidi added.

DS Elliot sighed, either disappointed with the men for not attending, or the women for attending for the wrong reasons.

"You wouldn't understand," Maggie told him gently, "you didn't know Lydia."

"Was she really so terrible?" he asked.

"Yes," the answered in unison.

"But you still want to catch her killer?" he queried, his brow furrowed.

"Well you can't have a murderer running around the place!" Maggie chastised.

"Or a thief or a blackmailer," Heidi added reasonably.

"Alright, that's fair. Any idea who this person might be? Did you find anything out at the funeral?" he asked again.

"You first," Heidi insisted.

"Me first, what?"

"What new information do you have?" she pressed.

"I can't share details on an ongoing investigation," he told her.

"Alright then, neither can I."

"Heidi! I mean- Miss Cross," he exclaimed, looking immensely uncomfortable.

"You can call her Heidi dear," Maggie told him, "but you really should tell us what you know, it is only fair if you want us to share information with you."

"Alright, fine, we don't have anything new. The items found at the pawn shop turned out not to be from Cross street," he admitted.

"Well that makes sense, since the items are being returned," Maggie offered.

"What?! What do you mean they're being returned?! By who?!" he demanded, looking around at them in obvious frustration.

"By the thief presumably. Money and stolen items are being returned."

Maggie spoke calmly, but DS Elliot appeared to be turning purple.

"Why didn't you tell me this?!"

"We're telling you now dear."

"When did items start reappearing?" he asked, forcing the words out through a tightly clenched jaw.

"Oh just in the last few days," Maggie told him

vaguely, waving one hand as though it weren't of the least interest.

Heidi watched, delighted as DS Elliot struggled to retain control.

"And no one thought this might be useful information for me to have?" he hissed.

"We've been busy dear! Our lives don't revolve around you you know!" Maggie chastised, drawing a wide grin from Heidi.

"Have you had anything returned?" he asked, pulling out his notebook and pen.

"A bell."

"I'll need to take it to check for finger prints," he stated, causing the smile to drop from Heidi's face.

"What?" he asked, when his words were met with nothing but uncomfortable glances in Heidi's direction.

"It was her father's," Shelley whispered, as though Heidi wouldn't hear her from ten inches away.

"It's alright, you can take it," Heidi told him in a small voice.

"But- I-" he floundered, clearly wishing that he could change his mind.

"You have to," she reminded him, "I'll give it to you before you leave."

He nodded briefly, his expression still a mix of pain and remorse.

"People have had money returned too," Heidi told him, keen to move the conversation on.

"And no one showed up to collect the blackmail money from the florist," he mused aloud.

"It seems that Lydia's death may have caused our thief to have a change of heart," Maggie suggested.

"I don't know," Heidi murmured slowly.

"What? What else could it be?" Shelley questioned, clearly fond of the idea of a remorseful and repentant killer.

"Well, it's just- it's not like Lydia's death was an accident. It didn't look like there was a struggle, or a fight or anything. She was stabbed in the back! That seems pretty intentional and cold blooded to me! Does that sound like the actions of someone who might change their mind?" Heidi asked them, really looking for an answer.

"No, no it doesn't," Maggie agreed.

"But then, why are they giving back everything they stole?" Shelley asked.

"That's a very good question," DS Elliot noted.

"Maybe, now that it's a question of murder, they don't want to be found with anything that could tie them to it?" Maggie suggested.

"Possibly, but there must be easier ways to get rid of stolen goods. Why risk being caught returning them?" Heidi asked.

No one had an answer for her this time.

"So aside from items being returned, is there anything else new?" DS Elliot asked them.

"I spoke to Mr Darcy," Heidi told them, "it seems that he actually knew Lydia through her husband. They knew each other as children, but they're definitely not friends. He sounded like he really *hated* him!"

"And hated Lydia by extension perhaps?" Maggie asked, an eyebrow raised.

That would be a nice solution, Heidi mused. If Mr Darcy, the unpleasant outsider could turn out to be the killer, then their Cross Street community would remain intact.

"He hasn't been around long enough to be the thief," Heidi pointed out, glumly.

"Shame," Maggie commented, clearly sharing Heidi's sentiments.

"One thing that he did tell me, was that he knew Lydia as Lydia Wickham," Heidi reported.

"Wickham? Was that her maiden name?" Shelley asked.

"Apparently not! He thought that started with B."

"Then why was she going by Wickes? Where did that come from?" Maggie asked, her voice dripping with suspicion.

"I have no idea," Heidi admitted, turning to DS Elliot.

He sighed, tapping his pen against his notebook to buy himself time.

"I suspect she was trying to make it harder for anyone to track her down," he told them finally.

"Track her down?! Who?!" Heidi demanded.

"You've been holding out on us!" Maggie cried.

"I don't have much concrete yet, but the officer who's been looking into Lydia Wickes' background has identified certain... irregularities. It seems that she burned a lot of bridges and racked up a lot of debts."

Maggie and Heidi turned to one another immediately to determine the value of this information.

"Could this be connected to her death?" Maggie asked.

"Hmm... probably not directly," Heidi told her.

"Why not?"

"Because if the killer is the thief, then it has to be someone from Cross Street. If Lydia knew someone here for years, we would know about it," Heidi explained.

"True. Unless they kept it secret, but why would they?" Maggie mused.

"Lydia might have reason to hide it, if she owed them money or betrayed them in some way-" Heidi began.

"But not the other party. Agreed."

Both satisfied that they had sorted through the information, they turned back to the group at large.

"Anything else you've neglected to share?" Maggie asked DS Elliot, her expression dark.

"No! I mean- no," he trailed off, flustered and not entirely convincing.

"Well we have nothing else either," Heidi told him.

"Really? You must have talked to a lot of people at the funeral, are you sure you didn't-"

"I'll fetch you the bell now," she told him, not allowing him to finish.

If he wasn't telling them everything, there was no way that she was going to betray Elizabeth and risk getting her in trouble.

She took him to where the bell rested, in its usual spot behind the till, but when the moment came for him to take it, she reached out in an involuntary motion and caught his arm. He looked at her quickly, in obvious surprise- not at her reluctance, but at the unexpected contact.

"Sorry," she murmured, pulling her hand away again.

"I'll be very careful with it, and I'll get it back to you as soon as I can," he told her softly, gently lifting her bell in one gloved hand.

She looked away, not wanting to see it go. Sensing this, he slipped out of the shop without another word, leaving Heidi stranded by the desk alone.

"Is he gone?" Maggie called from her armchair.

"Yes," Heidi barked back, her voice hoarse.

"Good. Now come back here and tell us what else you found out at the funeral."

Chapter 16

Heidi filled Maggie and Shelley in on Elizabeth's blackmail, but refused to get into a discussion about it. She didn't have the energy for speculation, she wanted nothing more than to crawl into bed and shut out the world for a few hours. Even Joan didn't put in an appearance to criticise her for attending the funeral that afternoon. Heidi was able to retreat to her room, and curl up with her book in peace until she fell asleep. The following morning however, was another matter. From the moment she awoke, her father kept up a constant string of questions that she couldn't answer, looping them round and round.

"Why would Lydia change her name? Why would someone attack her? Why would a thief return stolen property? Who could sneak into shops without being noticed?"

They were all good questions, but Heidi could feel them, making a knot of pain inside her skull.

"Ridiculous to be getting involved in all this!" Joan barked, causing the knot to tighten.

"I'm going for a run," Heidi informed them.

She knew that it was ridiculous, but she wanted a break. She needed to think things through on her own, even though technically, that was exactly what she *had* been doing. She changed into her running gear and set off, her feet pounding the pavement. It took a few minutes for her to realise that she wasn't watching the numbers on her running app. She wasn't counting steps either. Instead, she was replaying conversations from the last few days, looking for anything that didn't fit. She was sure that all the pieces were there, all the components of the story, she just needed to shuffle them into place. Something that Maggie had said snagged in Heidi's consciousness. If someone in Cross Street knew Lydia in the past, why would they keep it a secret?

Unless they both had something to hide.

Suddenly, pieces seemed to slot into place and a picture emerged. Heidi turned her steps and headed home. As soon as she entered the flat her father was there.

"It makes sense! It must be!"

"But how can I be sure?" Heidi asked him.

"Maybe talk to Rose? See if there are pictures?" he suggested.

"I'd rather not drag Rose into my suspicions again," she admitted.

"Alright, go to Mary! See if she can get you into

Lydia's flat! Maybe there's something there that can confirm it!"

Nodding with decision, Heidi turned to go, before catching sight of herself in the mirror. She was red faced, her hair glued to her scalp with sweat.

"Maybe a shower first," she mused.

It must have been the quickest shower of her life, and her hair was still wet, twisted up into a bun, when she started across the street towards Luscious Whisper. Mary was an early bird, always in the shop at the crack of dawn, getting ready for the day. Hopefully, Heidi could catch her before anyone else was around, and talk to her alone. She peered through the windows, but everything looked dark. Maybe Lydia's death and the murky question of inheritance, had caused Mary to take a step back from the shop. She tried the door, just in case, and was surprised to find it unlocked.

"Mary?" she called, pushing the door open.

Silence.

She moved further in, looking around the dark space. Maybe she could find something here. There might be some old family photos somewhere. She thought that she had seen a neatly concealed locker upstairs, when she'd been exploring with DS Elliot. Maybe Lydia had a picture on the inside of the locker door. That was something people did on television. The stairs were a striking feature, an open staircase leading from one side of the shop up to an open-plan second floor. Heidi walked towards it, but she couldn't go up, since Mary's body was blocking her path.

Maybe she really was cursed.

"Mary?" she called softly, her feet rooted to the floor. Nothing.

She forced herself to move forwards, though her every instinct was telling her to run. What if the killer was still here?! Concealed in the shadows of the unlit shop, anyone could be hiding!

But she couldn't leave Mary.

She edged forward, and knelt down, trying not to picture someone creeping up behind her. Mary's wrist was cold, but not in the way Lydia's had been. Heidi held it for a moment before-

There! A pulse!

Heidi let out a ragged gasp of relief and fumbled in her pocket for her phone.

"Hello, I'd like an ambulance please. And the police. To Cross Street. Not the bookshop this time, it's to Luscious Whisper. Yes, the lingerie shop."

Secure in the knowledge that help was on the way, Heidi tried to relax. She just had to keep Mary safe for a few minutes, until the police arrived. Surely she could do that.

The shadows seemed to stretch towards her as she waited, the darkness watching her with hungry eyes. By the time the shop door opened, Heidi was a mess of adrenaline and fear.

"Heidi?!"

DS Elliot entered and practically flew across the room, pulling Heidi into his arms. She let him hold her for just a second before pulling away.

"She's still alive! I asked for an ambulance," she told him quickly, kneeling back down beside Mary and very gently stroking her hair.

"Oh!" she exclaimed, pulling her hand away. It was red with blood.

"Well she didn't just fall down the stairs, did she," DS Elliot commented darkly.

Mary was loaded into an ambulance and driven away, and all Heidi could do was watch it go.

"I'll need your statement," DS Elliot told her gently.

She didn't respond, she didn't even hear him.

"Heidi? I- Miss Cross?" he ventured, searching her face for any sign that she was listening.

Eventually he touched her arm, causing her to start and turn to him guiltily.

"Sorry, did you say something?" she asked.

"I'll need your statement." he told her.

"Oh! Of course! Can we go to the bookshop? Or do I need to go to the police station this time? How many bodies can you find before the police have to bring you in for formal questioning?"

"There's no hard and fast number, and Mary isn't a body. You got her help, she's alive," he reminded her.

But Heidi's hand was still smeared with blood and Mary had been so cold and still.

"She must have been there hours," Heidi muttered.

"Why do you say that?"

"She felt cold. I think she'd been lying there since last night," Heidi explained, shivering involuntarily.

"Alright, let's go to the shop," he agreed, almost lifting an arm to wrap it around her, but stopping himself through sheer force of will.

Heidi hurried back across the street, with DS Elliot in tow, and was practically running by the time she reached the shop door. She let out a great sigh of relief when she crossed the threshold. Cross-Town Books felt like sanctuary. Thank goodness Mary hadn't been found here too, she didn't think she could cope with the shop being closed off again.

"Alright, talk me through everything that happened," DS Elliot prompted her, when she'd collapsed into her seat behind the desk.

"Nothing happened, I just walked across the street to

look for Mary and she was on the floor at the bottom of the stairs," she told him helplessly.

"Why were you looking for her?"

She hesitated, not sure how much to say. She certainly couldn't share her whole theory with him with no evidence, could she?

"I wanted to ask Mary if she'd seen any pictures that Lydia might have. Old pictures," she told him.

"Old pictures?" he pressed.

"I wanted to see if I might recognise anyone from Lydia's past. I was thinking about our conversation yesterday- if Lydia had such a... shady past, then maybe she was killed by someone who knew her years ago," she explained.

"I thought that you were sure she was killed by one of the residents of Cross Street?" he queried.

All she could do was shrug. She didn't want to tell him that she suspected that a significant figure from Lydia's past *was* a resident of Cross Street.

"Well Mary's very lucky that you did go looking for her! If you hadn't she wouldn't be on her way to the hospital now!"

Heidi let out a slow, shaky breath. Mary was on her way to the hospital. Because she'd been attacked. She was lying face down, at the bottom of the stairs, with a wound to the back of her head. Someone had hit her! Did that mean that she had important information and someone was trying to keep her quiet?!

"Is Mary safe?" she asked quickly.

"I've sent a couple of officers to meet her at the hospital. They won't leave her alone," he assured her, clearly having thought of this already.

"Have you had any luck finding Rose's father?" she asked, trying to keep her voice level.

"No, we think he must have changed his name, just like Lydia. We're still looking though."

"Any other new developments?" she asked hopefully.

"Nothing, I'm sorry. I'm sure we'll have something soon though. The bell is being checked for fingerprints, and maybe Mary will be able to tell us who..." he trailed off.

"Who attacked her? Someone is attacking people," she croaked, her voice sounding oddly hollow even to her own ears.

"Heidi, you can't keep looking into this. No more talking to people about Lydia. No more investigating," he told her firmly.

Heidi had actually been thinking just that, but for some reason his words made her bristle.

"Why not?!" she demanded.

"Because it's dangerous," he said simply, mystified by her annoyance.

"So?! That's exactly why it needs to be solved! We can't just let someone wander around attacking people!"

"We won't. I'm going to find them," he told her.

She crossed her arms over her chest but didn't answer him.

"I'm going to go to the hospital and check on Mary, would you like me to update you when I know how she is?" he asked her, forcing her to relax her stance and even thank him.

"And in the mean time, no detective work," he told her, throwing the words back over his shoulder as he left.

Heidi chose not to catch them.

DS Elliot didn't understand the situation, so of course he felt that she should leave the case to him. He didn't understand that, proof or no proof, Heidi was pretty sure she'd worked out who was behind everything. And he was dating Maggie.

There was still almost an hour until Maggie and Shelley were due to arrive at the shop, and Heidi used the time to plot out her theory. She noted down all the details, the coincidences of time, everything she could think of. Even to her, it didn't look like much, but she still felt so sure!

When Maggie walked through the door, Heidi was ready.

"It was Mr Darcy!"

Alright, she hadn't been ready. The words burst from her unbidden and Maggie stopped in her tracks, Shelley crashing into her from behind.

"Mr Darcy?!"

"It's his fault," Heidi amended.

"His fault?"

"Well, it's *because* of him," Heidi tempered further.

"So he's not the killer?" Maggie queried, looking crestfallen.

"No. No he's not. But it is partly his fault that Lydia is dead."

"How?" Shelley asked, shrugging out of her jacket and going to hang it up.

"Because he knew Lydia's husband. He was worried he was going to recognise him!"

Shelley stopped, frozen, jacket still in hand. Maggie gazed at Heidi in surprise and delight.

"Shelley's husband?!" Maggie cried excitedly.

"So it wasn't someone from Cross Street?!" Shelley added happily.

Heidi sighed. This wasn't going how she had hoped. She looked down at her notes and started to pace.

"It's alright dear, you go back to the beginning and we'll follow you from there," Maggie told her.

Shelley hung up her jacket and Maggie picked up her

duster, lightly flicking at the shelves to give Heidi time. She took a deep breath and tried to slow her thoughts down, following the guide she'd put to paper.

"Right, so, Mr Wickham changed his name. He came here, following Lydia to Cross Street. He opened his own shop, but it wasn't as successful as hers. To make ends meet, he started stealing from other shops. Then he started blackmailing people. He'd done things like this before, but then there was a problem. Mr Darcy showed up! He had known Wickham since they were children, he was obviously going to recognise him, and if it came out that he was secretly Lydia's ex-husband, pretending not to know her, he would be the obvious suspect for the crimes! He got spooked, and decided he needed to get rid of anyone who knew who he really was. The only name on that list was Lydia. He stabbed her, and put her body into one of the shops that he had made keys to. He couldn't go to the funeral, because Mr Darcy was there. But maybe he had really loved Lydia once, and they did have a child together, so her death was enough to make him regret everything. He started putting some things back in the other shops, but he was more worried than ever about people finding out who he was. He was worried there might be something connecting him and Lydia, in her shop. So he went over there last night to look, but Mary was still there, so he hit her in the back of the head and pushed her down the stairs." Heidi finished in a rush, her chest heaving.

"What?!" Shelley cried.

"Mary?!" Maggie clutched her own chest, her eyes wide.

"She's alive, I found her early this morning, she's at the hospital now. She was in bad shape though," Heidi admitted, chewing her lip, "when I first found her I thought she was..."

Maggie gave her a warm heavily scented hug. The sequins of her shawl prickled Heidi's arms but it still felt nice.

"So you think it's Alexander," Maggie concluded when she stepped back.

"Mr Price?!" Shelley exclaimed, having been too distracted by Mary's attack to follow Heidi's logic to its conclusion herself.

"He didn't go to the funeral," Heidi pointed out.

"And he is closer to Lydia's age than mine," Maggie added gloomily.

"That doesn't mean anything!" Shelley insisted.

"And I've always wondered how his business survives," Heidi admitted.

"Model planes and all his other oddities... he never does seem to have customers in there," Maggie admitted.

"But- but-" Shelley stammered helplessly.

"You really think he's Mr Wickham? You think he's the killer?" Maggie asked, squaring her shoulders.

"I do. I sort of suspected him all along, but this morning pieces started to really fit into place," Heidi told her.

"Is that why you went to Mary?" Shelley asked.

"I was hoping that Lydia might have some old photos that would prove it, and Mary might be able to help me find them. The shop was unlocked and when I went in-" Heidi broke off abruptly, shivering again.

"Poor Mary," Maggie sighed.

"DS Elliot went to the hospital. He promised to call me and let me know how she's getting on," Heidi told them, blushing despite the seriousness of the situation.

As one, their eyes turned to Heidi's phone on the counter. They watched it for a moment, but it didn't ring.

Chapter 18

"What do we do now? Did you tell DS Elliot about your suspicions?" Maggie asked.

"No, how could I? I don't have any proof," Heidi shrugged.

"We could ask Rose?" Maggie suggested tentatively.

"That wouldn't be fair. What if I'm wrong? Or worse, what if I'm right?!"

Maggie and Shelley both agreed with this sentiment wholeheartedly.

"What about pictures then? Your original plan from this morning," Maggie suggested.

"Luscious Whisper is closed off as a crime scene now. No one is getting in there and I doubt we'll be able to get into Lydia's flat even if we knew where she lived," Heidi told them.

"Only a few streets away, but you're right, we'd need a key," Maggie grumbled.

"There is one thing," Heidi began.

"Yes?!"

They both looked at her eagerly but Heidi wasn't sure she could go on.

"What is it?!" they demanded.

"Well- Maggie- I don't know exactly how close you and Mr Price have got- but is there any chance you've seen him with his shirt off?" she asked, cringing inwardly.

"I beg your pardon?!" Maggie exclaimed.

"Just his upper arms!" Heidi hastened to clarify.

"I most certainly have not!" Maggie announced, adjusting her shawl like a bird ruffling disturbed feathers.

"Are you sure?" Heidi pressed.

"Young lady, I know your generation moves at warp speed, but I have a little more decorum," she insisted gravely.

"Alright, that's that then," Heidi sighed.

"Why? What would it have meant if Maggie had seen his arms?" Shelley asked.

"Mr Wickham has a tattoo of Lydia's name on his upper arm. It's one of the only things Rose remembers about him. If he had the tattoo, we would know it was him!" Heidi explained.

They all lapsed into thoughtful silence.

Eventually, blushing profusely, Heidi looked at Maggie again and ventured a suggestion.

"I don't suppose you would..."

"I most certainly would not! Heidi Cross, who do

you think I am?! Mata Hari?!" Maggie demanded, outraged.

"Alright, Alright! Sorry!" Heidi quickly apologised, "I don't know what we do next then."

"We find another way to glimpse Alexander's upper arms," Maggie told her with a sigh.

After an hour of muttering to one another and casting furtive glances at the door, the plan was simple. Whether it would actually work, they had no idea, but they were prepared to try. The first step was to get Alexander round to the bookshop.

"Maybe he'll come in anyway! He often does!" Shelley pointed out, not for the first time.

"But we can't rely on that! What if he doesn't?" Heidi told her again.

"But what if I make a mess of it?" Shelley pleaded.

"You wont! Just run through it again dear, from the top," Maggie told her.

"Alright, I go around the block, so it looks as though I'm just arriving at work. I stop at Mr Price's shop on the way, stick my head in and ask if he's heard about Mary," Shelley intoned.

"And then?"

"I give no details. I say I have no idea, but apparently Heidi knows all about it. I tell him to stop by this morning and I'll have some cakes so we can all have a sit down together."

"Perfect!" Maggie told her.

"But I've never done anything like that before! I've never invited him to the bookshop, or stopped to gossip, or anything! Isn't he going to be suspicious?!" Maggie asked them.

"No one has ever been attacked or murdered in the shop before either. I suspect we're all acting slightly out of character," Maggie reassured her.

"Just make sure you don't go into the shop. Don't be alone with him. Be careful! If he tries to get you to enter the shop, say you need to get to work and just come straight here," Heidi told her firmly.

After a couple more minutes of nerves, and a few more repetitions of the plan, Shelley set off, jogging up the street. Heidi and Maggie watched her go until she was out of sight, and then they busied themselves with the everyday routine of the shop. They still didn't have a single customer, but the shelves would always need dusting and there were more than enough of those to keep the two of them busy until Shelley returned.

She burst through the shop door ten minutes later, looking triumphant but harassed.

"I was not built for subterfuge!" she hissed.

Heidi thought that these words were entirely unnecessary, as no one looked *less* duplicitous than the petite, freckled single mother in the flip flops, standing in front of her.

"But it worked?" Maggie asked eagerly.

"Yes, he said he'd come in around lunch- earlier if he could manage it. He definitely seemed interested! *I* was a complete moron though! I couldn't make my voice sound natural at all! I was all high pitched and ridiculous!"

Maggie and Heidi beamed at her.

"Fantastic job dear! On to stage two!"

Shelley didn't look particularly enthusiastic. Stage two was infinitely more precarious than stage one, and it led directly into a highly risky and awkward stage three, but Heidi couldn't help it, she was excited.

"We need cakes!" Maggie declared, happily.

She swept from the shop and returned just minutes later with a selection of pastries, cakes and eclairs.

"At least this ghastly plan has snacks," Shelley grumbled, surveying the assorted treats.

The coffees would be Heidi's responsibility. They didn't want take away cups with lids, so Heidi was making a batch of coffee herself, to be drunk chilled, over ice. She nipped upstairs to her flat and got it ready, bringing it down on a tray, with five open glasses.

"What about DS Elliot?" Maggie asked.

"I sent him a message, but I expect he's busy. I'm sure it'll be fine if he doesn't come though. I don't mind either way," Heidi babbled, setting her tray of coffee down on the counter.

"I see you've brought him a glass though," Maggie pointed out, clearly amused.

"Well that's just polite!" Heidi insisted, adjusting the containers so that they were all spaced evenly on the tray.

Just a few minutes later, DS Elliot did put in an appearance, but he didn't look exactly thrilled about it.

"What's all this about a plan?" he demanded immediately, frowning around at them.

"First things first, how's Mary?" Maggie asked him.

"She's still unconscious, and she's pretty banged up, but the doctors are hopeful. She should be awake soon and then we might have a solution to all this," he told them, gesturing around to their group, the shop, or maybe the street at large.

"Well that's a nice idea, but it's not exactly a certainty, is it?" Heidi pointed out.

"Well no, but it's better than nothing. And better than something dangerous. What's all this about a plan?" he demanded again.

"A plan to get proof," Heidi told him cheerfully.

"Proof?"

"Would you prefer vague and unsubstantiated suspicions?" Heidi asked him.

"Yes! Yes I would!" he insisted.

"Don't be ridiculous! Of course proof is better! Now, all you have to do is go away, and reappear at the right time, and you should see some proof," Heidi told him.

This explanation hadn't been particularly illuminating and Heidi wasn't surprised that DS Elliot was still glowering.

"I don't want to say anything more just yet, but if you follow the plan, it should help your investigation," she pleaded.

"What is this plan?" he asked with a sigh.

She rewarded him for this softening of his stance, with an iced coffee and a bun.

"You just need to go, somewhere close, and wait. Watch the bookshop, and when Mr Price comes in, wait five minutes and then come in. It'll be important that you enter the bookshop exactly five minutes after Mr Price," she explained.

"Why?"

"I'd rather not say."

He took some convincing, but when it became clear that they were going to go through with it no matter what he did, he relented. He slipped out of the shop to secret himself away out of sight and the three women took to hovering anxiously around the coffee tray.

Heidi had just opened her mouth to ask where on earth Mr Price could be, when the door chimed and he

267

walked in.

"My dear ladies!" he boomed theatrically.

Shelley started involuntarily, and Mr Price looked at her in concern.

"Are you alright dear?"

"She's just nervous!" Heidi told him quickly, "we all are, after what happened to Mary!"

"Yes, it's nice to have *you* here with us for a bit Alexander, I feel much safer," Maggie fluttered at him.

"My pleasure my dear," he told her, kissing her hand and bowing low.

"Such a gentleman!" Maggie twittered.

Heidi worried that she was slightly overdoing it, but Mr Price didn't seem phased, so perhaps this was what they were like when they were alone together.

"Speaking of poor Mary, I understand that you have the inside scoop?" he asked, turning to Heidi, "not to sound macabre of course!"

"It's not macabre, she's going to be fine," Heidi told him quickly.

Mr Price definitely seemed to start at these words, and Heidi watched him closely. Was she imagining things, or had his eyes flickered towards the door?

"Oh really?! Wonderful news! I was told that there had been another tragedy, and I suppose I let my imagination run away with me," he told them, shifting uncomfortably on the spot.

"Why don't we sit?" Heidi suggested brightly, wanting to keep Mr Price firmly fixed within the bookshop.

"A splendid idea! I'll bring the cakes!" Maggie cried, ushering Alexander into the armchair in the reading corner.

"I'm not sure how long I have-" he began, but Maggie pressed him ruthlessly into the seat and placed a chocolate eclair in his hand with determination.

"I feel so much safer with you here though, and you'll want to hear all about Mary, I'm sure!" she told him.

"Oh, yes- yes of course!" he agreed, taking a bite of eclair.

Shelley still stood in place, a faint look of concentration on her face as she counted seconds.

"I'll get the coffees!" Heidi suggested, earning herself a 'slow down' gesture from Shelley.

"And I'll tell you about Mary!" Heidi added.

"I found her this morning, at the bottom of the stairs in Luscious Whisper. She might have fallen down them, but she was alive! I called an ambulance-" she reported, aware that she was racing far too quickly through the story. She slowly poured a coffee over a cup of half melted ice and handed it to Maggie. She then poured a second, pausing to add to the story.

"When I walked in to the shop, it was so dark I could barely see her. She was just lying there on the floor. At first I thought she was dead, but when I felt her wrist I found a pulse," she told them, trying to slow her words. She picked up the second coffee and at a nod from Shelley, moved towards Maggie and Mr Price. She extended her hand, as though to pass him the drink, but then at the last moment, she tipped herself forward and threw the entire contents of the cup over him.

"Oh my gosh! I'm so sorry!" she cried.

"Alexander! My dear!" Maggie added, already fumbling with his shirt buttons.

"Good God!" he exclaimed, trying to rise, but being prevented by Maggie's ministrations, "It's fine! It's fine! I can go home and change!" he cried.

They ignored him.

"Don't worry! I can wash the shirt! The quicker the better, so it doesn't stain!" Heidi told him, helping Maggie with the buttons, as Mr Price tried to bat their hands away.

In the end they basically had to wrestle him out of the garment, but after a tense moment, they both stepped back triumphantly, just as the bell over the door chimed.

"There!" Heidi crowed, pointing to Mr Price's upper arms.

But they were bare.

Not a blemish, or a freckle, or a scar. Certainly not a tattoo, or any trace that there had ever been one.

Heidi felt almost as though she could see the scene, laid out. Mr Price, trapped in the armchair, red in the face and desperately trying to cover his bare chest. Heidi herself, frozen with a look of triumph, just turning to horror on her face, Maggie still clutching the coffee soaked shirt, Shelley watching in dismay, and DS Elliot bursting upon the scene in confusion.

"Can I ask what on earth is happening here?" he enquired, taking in the tableaux before him.

"I just spilt some coffee!" Heidi cried in a high, unnatural voice, desperately trying to broadcast to him that the plan was off.

"No tattoo!" Maggie cried, scuppering her endeavour.

"Tattoo?!" Mr Price demanded, grabbing his sodden shirt from Maggie and trying to pull it back on.

Heidi buried her face in her hands, realising that this must be what mortification feels like.

"Here, it really is too wet, you can wear this," Maggie told him.

Heidi emerged from her hands to find Mr Price bedecked in Maggie's spangled shawl and an expression of outrage.

"Why on earth were you looking for a tattoo?!" he demanded.

"A bet?" Maggie attempted feebly.

"It's my fault," Heidi admitted with a sigh, "Lydia's husband had her name tattooed on his upper arm."

Mr Price blustered for a moment before bursting out "you thought I was Lydia Wickes' husband?! Why?!"

He looked around at them all, waiting for an answer, before the full impact of the situation hit home.

"YOU THINK *I* KILLED HER?!" he boomed, causing them all to flinch.

"Just to be absolutely clear, I'm not involved with this," DS Elliot announced, maybe not pushing them under the bus, but certainly not helping them out of its way.

Heidi cast him a dark look but he held up his hands.

"I'm the *police*! I have to think of professional reputation!"

Heidi could have been wrong, but she thought she detected amusement in his tone.

"I am so sorry Mr Price!" Heidi told him, reaching to take the coffee stained shirt, "I really will wash this for you."

"No! Thank you but no!" he snapped coldly.

"I just thought- you see, when you didn't-" she stammered, not sure how to explain.

"I have no interest in your wild theories thank you very much! I have never been so insulted in all my life!"

He finally managed to push up out of the armchair, and, still clutching Maggie's shawl about his torso, he strode from the shop. No one spoke for a moment, and then suddenly, DS Elliot burst out laughing. They all joined him, it was contagious, and the ridiculousness of the situation struck them all. When the laughter subsided however, they all looked grave.

"Will he forgive you?" Heidi asked Maggie.

"Oh I expect so," she replied, but she didn't look convinced.

"I'm sorry Maggie," Heidi told her.

"Maybe I'll just go and try to have a word with him," Maggie told them, following after Mr Price with an anxious expression.

"I'm going to go to the dry-cleaners and see if there's a coupon or a voucher or something I can get him for his shirt," Shelley announced, grabbing her bag.

"Take the money out of the till!" Heidi told her.

When she was alone with DS Elliot, Heidi blushed. She wished that she'd never dared to include him in her plan.

"So what made you suspect him?" he asked lightly.

"He didn't go to the funeral. I thought he wanted to avoid Mr Darcy, in case he recognised him. And his business never seems to have customers, but he's still getting by. I thought he was stealing and blackmailing to make ends meet."

Saying it to Maggie and Shelley it had sounded so convincing, but repeating it now to DS Elliot it seemed paper-thin.

"A secret husband in disguise?!" she cried aloud, before burying her face in her hands again.

He couldn't help it, DS Elliot broke down into fresh laughter.

"It does seem more like dramatic fiction than real life," he noted.

"I suppose I have more experience of fiction than of real life," she admitted, throwing herself into the armchair and selecting a cake from the box.

"Because everybody died?" he asked gently, sitting across from her.

Her own words repeated back to her, without the sting of anger, made her chest tighten.

She shrugged, "my parents, and then my aunt who raised me."

"I'm sorry."

He really did sound sorry, and the honest sympathy so soon after the crippling embarrassment was almost enough to push her over the edge. She felt tears burning her eyes and took a large bite of cake, hoping to cover the moment. DS Elliot took a cake too, and for a while they were content just to eat together, allowing the silence to stand.

"This is nice," he commented.

"The cake?"

"No- well yes- the cake is very nice, but I meant eating with you," he explained.

"Oh."

She didn't know what to say. It *had* been nice until he'd said that! Suddenly though, she was feeling anxious, uneasy and wondering if she always chewed this loudly.

"Maybe we could eat together again this evening?" he suggested.

"What? This evening? To talk about the case?" she responded, lost at sea and desperately searching for solid ground.

"Um, yes, we could do," he reasoned.

"Or we could-"

"Alright. To talk about the case we could," she cut in, her voice small but sure.

"We could? We could!" he agreed happily, clearly deciding that this was a positive enough result that he wouldn't mess with it.

"I could pick you up here?" he suggested.

"But I usually eat early," she told him, suddenly rethinking and seized by doubt.

"How early are we talking?" he queried.

"I normally eat by six. It's healthier. Maybe we should just forget about-"

"I'll come get you after five! I'll come straight from work!" he insisted.

"Straight from work? So you might have updates," she mused.

"Exactly! I might have all sorts of new information on the case! And we could talk through what we already know," he told her, grinning.

He knew he had the upper hand in that respect, and Heidi was finding it difficult to resist. She wasn't entirely sure that she *wanted* to resist but she wasn't examining her own feelings too closely.

"Alright, I'll be here," she told him.

He beat a retreat before she could change her mind, passing Maggie in the doorway and exchanging a few words with her.

"A dinner?!" Maggie enquired when she reached Heidi.

"How's Mr Price?" Heidi countered.

"An actual dinner?! With a handsome young man?!" Maggie pressed on.

"Is he still angry? He's not angry with *you* is he? You told him it's all my fault?" Heidi asked.

"I think you're going to have a wonderful time

Heidi, and I'm very proud of you! Such a handsome young man!"

"Mr Price, Maggie! How is Mr Price?!" Heidi demanded.

"Such a handsome young man," Maggie muttered to herself in a satisfied manner.

The shop bell sounded and Shelley entered, bearing a piece of paper.

"What's going on?" she asked them.

"Apparently Mr Price is going to dinner with a handsome young man," Heidi snapped.

"What?" Shelley asked, looking bewildered.

"Well I keep asking about Mr Price and that's all Maggie will say!"

Shelley looked between them in evident confusion.

"Heidi is going to dinner!" Maggie explained.

"With DS Elliot?!" Shelley exclaimed, clapping her hands together.

"He's coming to get her after work," Maggie confirmed.

"What happened at the dry cleaners?" Heidi asked, stubbornly ignoring their discussion.

Both women stared at her happily, lost in their own daydreams, before Shelley finally shook her head slightly and snapped out of her reverie.

"I got a voucher for the dry cleaners," she told them,

"it's not really a service they offer but they made a voucher for me specially and printed it out. If Mr Price brings this in with his shirt, they'll clean it for him. We've already paid for it."

"Do you want to take the voucher round to him?" Heidi asked Maggie.

"No, no dear. I've already made my apologies, and promised to make it up to him and explain all about the mix-up this evening. You're the one who needs to win back some favour," she replied.

Heidi took the voucher with a sigh.

"I suppose I should. Do I just say sorry?" she asked anxiously.

"That's the idea, yes. You apologise, and hope he forgives you. It's one of the inconvenient aspects of socialising, but it is quite important," Maggie explained, ushering her out the door.

Chapter 19

As Maggie and Shelley dove into conversation, no doubt about Heidi's impending dinner, Heidi herself made her way slowly along the street. She practised a few apologies in her head, and, clasping the voucher in her hand, pushed open the door to Mr Price's shop.

It was even more eclectic than she remembered. It always seemed to have a mish-mash of wares, but when Heidi was a child it had been a notably rare and high-class mish-mash. Now there were chess sets, figurines, packs of batteries, small tins of paints and varnishes, and countless model planes. Some were resting on shelves, and some were suspended from the ceiling. Heidi ducked slightly to avoid a small, two seater painted in white and red.

"Low hanging Cessna" she said aloud, her insides bubbling with nervousness.

"Mr Price!" she called, forcing her voice to rise about a whisper.

She waited but no one appeared. She studied the shelves, packed with paper-weights, key-chains, clocks and

Russian dolls. She was just nerving herself up to shout a little louder when she heard footsteps overhead. The footsteps moved towards the back of the shop, and were followed by the unmistakable sound of someone descending stairs in smart shoes.

"Heidi! What a pleasant surprise," Mr Price commented drily, upon seeing her.

"I'm sorry," she began quickly, holding out the voucher, "this is to cover the dry cleaning of your shirt. I'm really sorry!"

He took the voucher and visibly softened.

"I appreciate that," he told her, stowing the voucher behind the counter.

"It was all just me getting carried away and seeing things that weren't there," she told him.

"Such as?"

"I'm sorry?" she asked, confused.

"What made you think I was a murderer?" he asked bluntly.

Heidi didn't know what to say. She certainly couldn't lay out her theory that he was blackmailing and stealing to support his business because he didn't have any customers!

"Well, you didn't go to the funeral," she told him lamely.

"I didn't feel comfortable attending. Lots of people didn't. Miss Wickes was a very unpleasant woman," he told her, studying her closely.

"Yes, that's true," she squirmed, "but you told Maggie you would come, so when you didn't I just..." she trailed off, not knowing how to finish.

"I had work to do. I do a lot of business by post. Collectors, you know."

"Well, I'm sorry, I just got carried away," she told him again.

"I quite understand. This has been a difficult situation for all of us. We don't like to think of a killer in our midst."

His words were understanding but his voice was still cold. Heidi resigned herself to this apology being an ongoing endeavour.

"Well, I am sorry. Hopefully I'll see you around," she told him, shuffling on her feet.

"Quite. I'm sure you will," he told her, not particularly reassuringly.

She turned to go and almost collided with the small plane again. She had to step around it to make her way to the door, blushing again to the roots of her hair.

He didn't speak again until she had the door open and was about to go,

"I do appreciate you apologising Heidi. Thank you. And that's a De Havilland by the way, not a Cessna."

Heidi let out her breath in a great burst when she got

outside. After the darkness of the shop and the oppressive atmosphere created by Mr Price's anger, the bright sunshine and the quiet of Cross Street felt heavenly. She hurried back to the bookshop, steeling herself to deflect or ignore all questions about her dinner with DS Elliot. She was regretting ever having agreed to it in the first place.

"Heidi dear! How did it go?" Maggie asked when she entered.

"He's still angry," she announced.

"Who's angry?"

It was Rose who spoke. She had clearly come round to socialise, but Heidi couldn't possibly explain the whole situation to her.

"Mr Price. Heidi thought that he was " Maggie began.

"Stealing!" Heidi shouted, cutting her off.

"What?!" Rose exclaimed.

"Yes, I know, it's crazy. I don't know what was wrong with me," Heidi rushed on, "but I thought he might be the thief. He's not though!"

"Of course he's not!" Rose cried, looking deeply upset.

"I was just round there apologising," Heidi told her.

Rose calmed down a little at this, but she still looked worried. Heidi was glad that she hadn't told her she'd suspected Mr Price of being her father, and of killing her mother.

"How are you Rose?" she asked, noting the young woman's pale face and grave expression.

"I'm just tired. I'm still going through mum's flat, sorting out her stuff. It's been days and it doesn't feel like we've made any progress! I haven't been sleeping, and now with Mary..." she trailed off, running her hands through her hair.

"Oh you poor thing! Let us know if we can help at all! We could help sort through your mum's place-" Maggie began to offer, putting an arm around the young woman, but Rose flinched away.

"No! No, mum would want me to do it. I should be the one to do it. And Robert. He really has been amazing. He's such a fantastic guy!" she told them, finally smiling.

Heidi was surprised again at this complete turnaround. Rose had gone from doubting Robert and having definite suspicions about his involvement in the thefts, to suddenly having absolute confidence in him.

"I should get back to the bakery. We haven't had our usual mix of customers, but the residents of Cross Street have all been in in droves! I guess everyone is feeling the need for some comfort food," she told them, heading for the door, "I only stopped in to let you know Robert found my dad. He's living on some riverboat up north. He told him about mum, but... he didn't seem particularly interested apparently."

Maggie and Shelley waved her off as Heidi retreated to her usual spot behind the desk.

They had found Wickham. Just a few hours earlier and they might have avoided Heidi humiliating herself. She allowed herself to slump across the desk, staring at the empty space that used to be occupied by her father's bell. She hadn't worked out anything. She hadn't found the thief, the blackmailer, the killer who had terrorised the street. She hadn't helped Elizabeth, she had no idea where the mystery drugs could have come from or what she should do about them. She hadn't protected Mary from getting hurt. All she'd done was come up with a mad theory about a secret husband in disguise- a storyline out of a book! Not something from real life!

And now she was going to- what?

Have dinner with DS Elliot to talk through the details of the case?

She was playing detective, that's all, and this wasn't a game. She'd been questioning people and poking into their lives, and all the while danger had been closing in on Mary, and Heidi had no idea why.

Sitting there, dejectedly, as the afternoon wore on, Heidi became increasingly convinced that she needed to cancel the dinner with DS Elliot. She had nothing of value to add to the investigation, which made the dinner look alarmingly like a date.

Maggie was no fool, and she had known Heidi Cross all her life. She read the warning signs and took steps accordingly. By the time Heidi had worked up the nerve to call or message DS Elliot, he was already standing outside.

"What are you doing here?!" she asked, checking the time.

It wasn't even nearly five o'clock yet and she hadn't been expecting him for at least an hour.

"I decided that earlier is better," he told her with a grin.

"But- but-" she stammered helplessly.

"Come on! Maggie and Shelley have everything under control here," he told her confidently.

"Absolutely we do dear!" Maggie shouted in corroboration.

"But-"

"You did say that you're an early eater," he pointed out.

"But-"

"We can mind the shop! You go!" Shelley added.

She looked around at them all. Shelley, trying to look reassuring, but smiling widely. Maggie beaming and waving her off. DS Elliot grinning disarmingly. She admitted defeat.

"Do I need to change?" she asked with a sigh.

"And let you escape up to your flat? Not a chance. You look perfect," he told her.

She was in one of her mother's floaty skirts and a white blouse edged with daisies. She did like her outfit, it was actually one of her favourites, so she supposed it would do.

"Where are we going?" she asked, picturing a dimly lit restaurant, the air heavy with expectation and the choking scent of artificial fragrance.

"We're going to have a picnic. We'll sit outside, eat some food, talk," he told her brightly, "it's a lovely day!"

That sounded a thousand times better than a restaurant, but Heidi couldn't see any food. She wondered whether their first step was going to be a supermarket. Would that make this less like a date? Would she be disappointed if it did?

Chapter 20

She followed him in silence, as he walked to the end of the road and set off down another street and then another. After a couple of minutes, they came to a small deserted road and he stopped at a plain, black car. It was only when he fished out a set of keys that she realised it must belong to him. She wanted to ask if he lived in this road, but she was worried he might read something in to it.

"Are we driving somewhere?" she asked instead.

"Nope."

Instead of getting in to the car, he went straight to the boot and opened it. Heidi edged closer warily, thoughts of Ted Bundy running through her mind. If she was murdered and stuffed into the boot of a car, Maggie would notice. She and Shelley would point the authorities straight at DS Elliot. Luckily, this theory would not need to be tested out, as instead of a murder weapon, DS Elliot pulled out a large canvas backpack and shut the boot again.

"Come on!" he told her, setting off on foot in the opposite direction from the way they had come.

He led her to a nearby park. It wasn't one of the large, sprawling green spaces preferred by the tourists and masses of students, it was a much smaller affair, bordered on two sides by brick walls ornamented by climbing roses.

"I've never been here," she told him, looking around her.

"I thought not. I come here a lot, I have for years. It's a memorial park for a Gillian Thompson," he told her.

"Who's Gillian Thompson?"

"I have no idea, she died before I was born, but it's a lovely park, isn't it?"

She had to agree. It was peaceful without being too quiet. It was actually somewhere between a small park and a large garden, with it's flowers and bushes.

"Now, would you prefer to sit on a bench, or on the floor? I have a blanket if you'd like to sit on the grass. It is traditional for a picnic," he told her with a shrug.

She did quite like the idea of sitting on the floor, but she looked anxiously at his smart trousers.

"I'm not sure you're quite-" she began.

"Floor it is!" he announced, pulling a blanket from the backpack and spreading it out on the ground.

He sat down before she could argue and started pulling food from the bag. He had brought crisps, cans of soft drink, thick sandwiches, filled with ham, mozzarella, pesto and salad, and an assortment of pastries and cakes in paper bags.

"This looks amazing," she told him, settling herself onto the blanket beside him.

"I know all the best places to buy picnic food," he told her conspiratorially, "one of my cousins is married to a baker who supplies a few cafes. She is, hands down, the best cook and baker I've ever met. She solves crimes too."

"Sorry?!" she exclaimed, laughing.

"She does! Professional baker, turned amateur sleuth!" he cried theatrically, offering her a sandwich.

She searched his face, trying to work out whether he was teasing her.

"She solves crimes?" she repeated uncertainly.

"Yep! She just sort of fell into it. I've heard all the stories of the murders she's solved. That's why I joined the police actually! When I heard the first story, about her dad finding a body in the woods... I knew what I wanted to do!" he admitted, blushing slightly.

Heidi felt a slight tug in her chest at the sight of his flushed face, but she wasn't sure what it was.

"That's nice," she muttered in a small voice, her eyes fixed firmly on her food as she began to eat.

"Why did you want to be a detective?" he asked.

Heidi jumped slightly. She'd forgotten that she told him that- it wasn't something that she usually talked about. In fact, she wasn't sure that she'd ever told anyone else that at all!

"Was it the puzzle? The justice?" he pressed.

"The excitement," she told him with a wry smile, "I liked the idea of rushing about, finding clues, piecing together the mystery."

"Breaking into businesses in the dark, to look for blood?" he asked her, one eyebrow raised.

It was her turn to blush.

"I didn't find any though, did I," she murmured.

"No, but you found that there wasn't any," he pointed out.

"What good is that?"

"Well investigating isn't all about being on the right track. Sometimes it's about closing off the wrong one," he explained.

"Well I definitely did a lot of that today."

"Which is progress!" he insisted, smiling.

She sighed, not able to put her thoughts into words.

"Come on, go through it with me. What do we know?" he asked her.

"Someone killed Lydia Wickes."

"Yes, alright, we do know that, but go back to the beginning. You need all the information you have, to form a theory. And only things you're sure of at first, not things you just suspect," he told her.

"Alright, we know someone was getting into locked

shops without breaking windows or doors. We know they were stealing things. Money, flowers, treasured possessions. We know they were finding people's secrets and blackmailing them. We know that Lydia threw a party to impress Mr Darcy and Mr Bingley, and that after the party she was in my shop, maybe confronting the thief. We know she was killed." Heidi reported the facts as though she were reading them off a list. No embellishing or guess work, just the things they knew for sure.

"I know its not a secret, disguised husband, but its still a pretty good story!" DS Elliot noted, "I mean, a mysterious thief, a body in a bookshop, and a misunderstood murder victim. Lydia sounds like a really complex person."

This grated on Heidi. Lydia? Complex?! Misunderstood?! Not in a million years. Only someone who had never met Lydia themselves could say that. Heidi pressed on.

"We know that Mary thought Lydia was leaving her the shop. We know that Lydia didn't want Rose and Robert to get married," she fired off.

"That's a good point... Robert. We're still looking into him, he doesn't have an alibi," DS Elliot cut in thoughtfully.

"No! Rose is sure he had nothing to do with any of this!" Heidi insisted.

"She's sure? How?"

"I don't know, but she is. She had suspicions when I first suggested it, but not any more."

"That's strange," DS Elliot commented.

He was right. Heidi had thought the same thing. One minute Rose was racked by doubts and the next she was completely certain that Robert was in the clear, that he couldn't possibly have been the thief. Heidi was sure that there was something there. She could feel pieces dropping into place.

"At least one part of this is a *really* good story for you," DS Elliot commented, "Lydia's redemption is worthy of a novel! By all accounts she makes a very unlikely hero, but she confronted the thief when they broke into your shop!"

Heidi froze. Lydia was a very unlikely hero. In fact, she was an impossible hero. Confront someone in the middle of the night because they were going to steal from the bookshop?! Never!

"Never. It doesn't make sense," Heidi muttered.

"Well people are surprising," DS Elliot commented.

"And then there's the drugs," Heidi mused aloud, no longer aware of the small park or of DS Elliot's puzzled expression.

"Drugs?" he asked quickly.

"Someone has been selling drugs in the street.

Someone was having them delivered to their shop. Maybe the thief? Or maybe not," she muttered.

"Drugs?! In the street with the murder?! Who?! Why don't I know about this?!" DS Elliot demanded uselessly.

"And the flowers... what were they? I'm sure Kitty said..."

"Go back to the drugs! Who has drugs?!" DS Elliot pleaded.

"ORCHIDS!"

Heidi roared the word, catching both herself and DS Elliot by surprise.

"Orchids?" he asked, his voice thin and defeated now.

"Orchids were her favourite flower!" Heidi explained, utterly elated.

She beamed at him, waiting for it all to click into place, but he didn't have all of the pieces she did, and he couldn't make out the picture.

"I'll explain, I will, I just need to check something," she told him, pulling out her phone.

"Wait, you know who the killer is? Who the thief is?" he asked.

"Yes, and yes," she confirmed as the phone rang.

There was no answer. She tried again, but still no answer. Next she dialled Shelley, who thankfully picked up after just a few rings.

"Heidi? Is everything alright?"

"Um, yes, probably, I just can't get hold of Maggie. You don't know where she is, do you?" Heidi asked.

"Oh! Yes, after the shop closed for the day, she went round to Mr Price's. I think they're having dinner there so that she can fill him in on this morning," Shelley told her.

Heidi felt her heart sink.

"Thank you," she muttered, hanging up the phone.

"Heidi? Are you alright?" DS Elliot asked, studying her face.

"No. No I'm not. Maggie is with the killer."

These words acted like a starting pistol to Heidi. She jumped up and went to run, but DS Elliot caught her wrist.

"Hold up! I thought it wasn't Mr Price? Something about a missing tattoo?"

"I was wrong about that, I was wrong about a lot of things, but I was right about *who*! I think I know it all now! And Maggie is with him *right now*, having dinner and filling him in on my suspicions! She's in danger!" Heidi explained, pulling her arm out of his grip and sprinting away.

Sandals are not made for running, but neither are smart, men's brogues, so Heidi was gone before DS Elliot could grab his bag and take off after her. She practically flew through the streets, dodging pedestrians and skirting cyclists. As she ran, she kept pressing the call button on her phone. One way or another, she had to reach Maggie!

She was just a few streets away when Maggie finally answered.

"Heidi Cross, don't make me regret putting my number in your phone! What on earth is going on?!"

Heidi screeched to a halt, looking back hopefully for DS Elliot, but he must have taken a different route, she couldn't see him anywhere.

"Maggie where are you?!" she demanded quickly.

"What business is that of your-"

"Are you with Mr Price?!" Heidi hissed, tears stinging her eyes.

"Well if you must know-"

"He's the killer."

There was silence on the other end of the phone. Heidi could feel her heart beating in her throat and it felt a little as though she might be sick, but she just clasped the phone to her ear and waited.

"Heidi, I have been working at Cross-Town Books for most of your life. I think I know how to lock up correctly! Frankly, disturbing my evening with Alexander just to check I've locked the bookshop to your satisfaction, is insulting! I'll see you soon enough Heidi, and then I expect an apology!" Maggie told her sternly.

This puzzling exchange was followed by a dull thud-

the sound of Maggie putting her phone down but not ending the call. Heidi could still hear her talking.

"That girl! She always needs to be in control!"

Next Mr Price's voice joined in, "How insulting! And what were you saying about this morning? Why did she suspect me?"

Heidi couldn't quite make out Maggie's reply, because she was already running again. Her sandals were starting to flap as the straps gave way, but she didn't slow down. She kept the phone pressed to her ear. She might not be able to make out Maggie's words, but she was sure that she would hear a scream or other signs of an attack. That was obviously why Maggie hadn't hung up! The whole spiel about Heidi not trusting her to lock up was just a ruse, a way to buy time and not let Mr Price know that they were on to him. Maggie was buying time for Heidi to reach her.

Should she hang up the phone? Heidi wasn't sure. Perhaps she should be calling the police! But that would mean disconnecting the call with Maggie, leaving her completely alone with Mr Price, and giving up their only advantage.

Besides, if DS Elliot trusted her at all, the police were already coming! Or at the very least... one police officer was.

As she approached Mr Price's shop, she forced herself

to slow down. She needed a plan, she couldn't just burst in there. She tried to slow her breathing and focus on what she could hear. Maggie and Mr Price must have moved further away from the phone, because although she could hear that they were still talking, it was muffled and faint. It didn't sound distressed at all, no indication that some epic battle was taking place, but Heidi couldn't hear anything to indicate what was actually happening.

She peered through the shop windows, but there was no movement within- they must both be upstairs in Mr Price's flat. She pushed tentatively at the shop door, but it didn't budge. Mr Price had told them all that he had his locks changed, but studying it closely, it looked scuffed and old, just like the rest of the door. Without hesitating, Heidi sprinted back up the street, stopping at the bakery and banging on the door. She kept banging until an alarmed looking Rose appeared and unlocked it.

"Heidi? What-" she began.

"I need the key to Mr Price's shop! Do you have it with you?!" Heidi cut in, working her hands in her frustration.

"What?! I don't- I-" Rose stammered helplessly.

"There's no time Rose! Maggie's in there with him! I have to help her!" Heidi cried, her voice dropping into a wail.

Rose studied Heidi's face for just a moment, before

rushing to her bag and fumbling through it. After a few seconds she gave up on her trembling fingers and turned the bag upside down, emptying the entire contents onto the floor. She scooped up a large ring of keys, flicking through it and separating one labelled "Price". She handed this over and the two young women looked at each other, not sure what to say.

"Well go one then," Rose finally offered, with a defeated shrug.

"It'll be alright!" Heidi told her, before turning and running again, the phone in one hand and the key in the other.

She held her breath as she inserted the key into the lock, but it worked! The key turned and she was able to ease the door open! She reached up one hand and held the clapper of the bell to keep it from sounding, and then she slipped into the dimly lit shop. Looking around this time, she noticed much the same as on her previous visit- shelves stacked with seemingly random knick-knacks and disconnected items. Now however, she gleaned the significance. Cheap wares, just taking up space to make the shop look serviceable, while the real business was all done by post and had nothing whatsoever to do with model planes.

Heidi pressed the phone to her ear but she still couldn't hear what they were saying. This wasn't going to work!

As she moved further into the shop, her attention still fixed on the phone, she forgot the low hanging model plane and collided with it with a clatter. She caught it quickly in her free hand but it was too late, there was no way they wouldn't have heard that upstairs! Sure enough-

"What was that?" she heard clearly, in Mr Price's voice, in her ear.

She couldn't hear Maggie's reply, but she didn't need to, she was formulating a plan. If she could lure Mr Price downstairs, away from Maggie, she should be able to keep her friend safely separated from the killer until the police arrived.

Carefully letting go of the plane, so that it hung back on it's string, she looked around for something else.

There! An assortment of heavy paperweights!

She selected one and carefully picked it up and put it down again with a clunk. She listened closely through the phone, but all was silent as Maggie and Mr Price listened to the noises downstairs in the shop. She tapped a couple of metal figurines together to create a metallic clang, and heard Mr Price ask "what the hell is going on?!"

After picking up and setting down a few more items, Heidi finally heard footsteps shifting overhead. She kept her fingers tightly crossed, that Mr Price would come down alone, and a couple of minutes later she was rewarded with the sight of him edging into the shop, his eyes scanning the space anxiously.

"Heidi! What on earth are you doing here?!" he exclaimed.

"Mr Price! How lovely to see you," she told him, with a bright smile.

"How did you get in?" he demanded, casting a swift glance at the door and narrowing his eyes.

"I'm surprised you came down, you should have just checked the cameras," she told him, keeping her tone light but watching closely to see how her words landed.

He narrowed his eyes still further and she saw his hands clench into fists, a muscle twitching in his jaw.

"I'm sure I don't know what you mean," he snapped.

"Oh yes you do. You have cameras in your shop Mr Price. And microphones too. You've had them for some time, to help you protect your... business" she told him, laying heavy emphasis on the last word.

"What are you talking about?!" he spat, his face contorted in anger.

"I'm talking about drugs Mr Price."

Her words hung in the air as they both remained stock still. Eventually Heidi pressed on.

"It's very disappointing. I was hoping for a secret husband, or at least a dark shared history, but no. Drugs."

"You can't prove that," he sneered.

"No, but Lydia could. Couldn't she?" Heidi whispered, feeling herself start to tremble.

The atmosphere in the shop was darkening by the second. The shadows creeping closer and setting the hairs on Heidi's neck on end. With every word, Mr Price's facade fell away and he began to look like a stranger.

"Yes, Lydia Wickes could prove it. And look what happened to her!" his face twisted into a smile as he spoke and Heidi felt a chill run down her back. Every instinct was telling her to run, but if she did she'd be leaving Maggie trapped upstairs with him. Instead, she stood her ground, doing her best to look calm and collected.

"You stabbed her in the back. That's what happened to her."

"She had it coming," he replied lightly.

"Did she?! Does anyone really have being stabbed in the back coming?!" she demanded.

"She was stealing, prying, sneaking around and looking into my private affairs," he told her flatly, the implication clear.

"Just like I am?" she offered.

"You should have left it alone," he told her, taking a step forward.

"And what about Maggie?" she asked, glancing quickly towards the window.

Where on earth were the police?!

"What about her?" he snapped.

"What's going to happen to her?" Heidi pressed.

"That is a shame, but unfortunately thanks to you, I have no choice. Perhaps you really are cursed."

"How can you possibly think you're going to get away with this?!" she demanded.

"I have to at least try," he told her, "this is my life!"

As he spoke, he drew forth a knife and Heidi felt her heart skitter and stop. Her blood pounded in her ears, deafening, completely blocking out all sound.

"DON'T YOU DARE!"

The screech came from nowhere, closely followed by a frying pan.

"Maggie?!" Heidi cried, "get back upstairs!"

But the frying pan Maggie had thrown had made a direct hit, colliding with the back of Mr Price's shoulders, sending him staggering forwards, and Maggie had a second pan still clasped in her hands.

"Not a chance!" she hissed, keeping her eyes fixed on Mr Price and the knife.

He straightened up quickly, rounding on Maggie with an expression of fury. Heidi didn't even think about it, she just grabbed the closest object, a heavy glass paperweight in fetching shades of blue and green, and threw it. It hit him in the middle of the back, not causing much damage, but the second one bounced off his head.

Unsurprisingly, this made him stop and turn back towards Heidi. He made for her, brandishing the knife, but before he'd gone more than a couple of steps, he was hit in the back of the leg by a stapler, and when he turned, a hole-punch narrowly missed his face.

With a roar of rage, he started back towards Maggie again, stumbling now with the effects of multiple hits.

Now, Heidi realised that unless you are exceptionally lucky, you're unlikely to be able to incapacitate an armed killer with paperweights and stationery, and although she may not be cursed, she was far from lucky. However, not many people will be able to remain standing after a scale model of a De Havilland two seater plan hits them square in the face.

Heidi grabbed the plane and swung it with all her might. It flew in a graceful arc, at the full extreme of it's tether, until it collided with great force, knocking Alexander Price unconscious and dislodging at least two of his teeth.

As he finally crashed to the floor, the sound of what seemed to be a thousand sirens filled the air.

Heidi allowed herself a small smile. It seemed that DS Elliot did, indeed trust her. He burst on the scene with a decidedly wild look in his eyes and took in the absolute chaos at a glance.

"I'm going to need a full explanation of all this you

know?" he told Heidi severely.

"Oh my gosh! Are we going to be arrested for assaulting him?! But it was self defence!" Maggie cried, panic-stricken.

"Don't worry Maggie, there are hidden cameras in here. They have the whole thing on tape," Heidi told her wearily. She suddenly found that she was exhausted and was mortified to feel tears stinging her eyes.

"Tape?! How old are you dear?! Even *I* know no one uses *tape* any more! It's all clever boxes and remembery sticks!"

Heidi laughed at this, but one of her legs seemed suddenly inclined to give way beneath her.

DS Elliot was by her side in a second, holding her up with one arm.

"Are you alright?" he asked anxiously.

"No, I ruined these sandals," she reported sadly.

"Oh no! And they're so pretty!" Maggie lamented.

DS Elliot looked between them in obvious exasperation.

"You two are absolutely mad!" he told them.

"Yes, quite possibly dear, but all the best people are!"

This time Heidi was indeed invited along to the police station to make her statement. It turned out that finding bodies on the floor of shops was one thing, but putting them there yourself, however justified, was quite another. Since Mr Price was still alive, if somewhat injured, it was all very civilised. Heidi gave the details of the encounter and some other details that she had neglected to share previously, and once the footage from Mr Price's own cameras confirmed her story, she was allowed to leave.

DS Elliot had a junior officer drive her home, since he was going to be busy for some time, but he promised to visit her the following day for what he called, "her grand finale".

Chapter 21

As good as his word, DS Elliot arrived at the shop at nine the next morning and was horrified to find it already open.

"You should be resting!" he cried from the doorway, seeing Heidi contentedly sipping her iced coffee as she dusted already spotless shelves.

"Why?"

"You had a showdown with a killer yesterday! That would earn a normal person a day off!" he told her, earning only a shrug in response.

"Honestly Heidi, are you alright?" he asked her, coming towards her and dropping his voice in a way that made Heidi's stomach feel strangely unsettled.

"Of course she's alright!" Maggie declared from the doorway, "Our Heidi is made of strong stuff!"

Seeing the people following in Maggie's wake, Heidi suspected that she might need to be.

Rose was visible over Maggie's shoulder, along with Robert, Kitty, Jane, and at least a dozen other residents of Cross Street. They filed in and made their way, chattering excitedly, to the reading corner. It was a strange sight, all the bean bags were filled with adults, eagerly watching Heidi as though waiting for the next chapter of a book to be read aloud.

The sound of the bell made them turn and cries of delight erupted at the appearance of Mary, supported on Elizabeth's arm.

As the clamour to greet their almost-fallen neighbour got underway, Heidi grabbed Elizabeth and muttered a quiet apology to her.

"Are you kidding?!" Elizabeth laughed, "You solved it! You saved us! And the police know everything so Jane and I aren't in any trouble!"

She flung her arms around Heidi and the young woman felt the last of her anxiety slip away. This delightful sensation lasted just a few minutes, until Maggie called out to the whole group to sit down and pay attention, so that Heidi could explain how she'd worked it all out.

"Sorry?" Heidi squeaked.

"It's your Poirot moment dear!" Maggie insisted.

"But you're going to help me, aren't you?!"

"How? I have no idea what actually happened! If you need help for the end bit, I'll join in then," Maggie told her, settling herself comfortably in her seat.

All eyes were on Heidi, watching her with interest. She swallowed hard, her mouth suddenly dry. As she ran through possible excuses for escaping up to her flat until everyone forgot about her entirely, she caught DS Elliot's eye. He was leaning against the nearest wall, watching her with a smile, one dimple curving his cheek. He winked and she felt a trickle of confidence. Even if she made a total hash of it, she had a feeling that things would be alright.

"Ok," she began tentatively, "I suppose it all starts with the break-ins."

"I can't believe Mr Price was stealing from everyone!" Shelley piped up indignantly.

"He wasn't," Heidi corrected her, making almost everyone start with surprise.

"He wasn't?!" Maggie demanded.

"Nope."

"Then he wasn't the blackmailer either?!" Maggie added.

"No. In fact, Mr Price was being blackmailed too. That's why all of this happened," Heidi explained.

"Then who was the thief? Who was the blackmailer?! They're not still out there are they?!" Elizabeth asked anxiously.

"No," Heidi told them all, looking uncertainly at Rose.

"It's alright," the young woman told her, "you can tell them."

They all looked from Heidi to Rose and back again,

realisation dawning on a few faces.

"It was Lydia," Heidi said simply, "that's actually how I worked everything out. DS Elliot said something about what a good story it was- Lydia confronting the thief for breaking into the bookshop. He said she was an unlikely hero."

A few of them scoffed at this.

"Exactly! Lydia just wasn't like that! If she had seen someone breaking into the bookshop, she wouldn't have done a single thing about it! She wasn't the sort of person who would step in to help somebody else, but she was the sort of person who would steal. The sort of person who would snoop. The sort of person who would take money from her neighbours, look into their business, exploit their secrets and steal orchids from the florist." Heidi reported.

"Her favourite flower!" Maggie cried excitedly.

Rose's head was bent in obvious shame and humiliation.

"I'm so sorry," she whispered to the group, her face flushed and her eyes bright with tears.

Robert took her hand, staring the group down defiantly.

Silence hovered in the air, thick and crackling, until Maggie broke it.

"That's alright dear. It's got nothing to do with you," she barked at Rose, always matter of fact.

"You're not responsible for her," Jane added sincerely.

The rest of them quickly added their agreement to this and Rose breathed a sigh of relief, tears flooding down her face.

"And you gave us our things back!" Heidi added, wanting to be sure that this point wasn't lost on anyone.

"What?" Shelley asked.

"The bell! The flowers! The money! Rose was the one who gave them back to us!"

"Of course I did! How could I not?!" Rose exclaimed, "when I started going through mum's flat I found everything. I realised that she must have been one the one stealing from everyone. I found the copies that she had made of everyone's keys. I knew I had to return everything I could."

There were a general babble of confusion around the topic of the keys, as not everyone had been present for Heidi and Maggie's theorising.

"We worked out that someone had been taking keys, making copies and returning them. A few people had lost their keys, but only temporarily so they hadn't thought anything of it. That was how we knew that the thief was someone who lives or works in Cross Street. They hadn't stood out, they were able to walk around all the shops without being noticed," Heidi explained.

"I say, that's very clever! Good reasoning!" piped up

Mr Bingley.

"So how did you figure out the rest?" asked Jane.

Heidi took a deep breath, not sure of where to start.

"Well, we'd narrowed down the suspect pool, it had to be someone from Cross Street. But that still left a lot of suspects. Lots of people hadn't liked Lydia. The real question was who had a good enough reason to kill her?"

"The police believed that she was killed as part of the competition for Mr Bingley's attention," Maggie burst out, cackling.

Mr Bingley wasn't the only one who coloured at her words, Jane turned a ladylike shade of pink and stared quickly down at the floor.

"What?!" Bingley demanded, horrified.

"Oh yes! A street full of mad ladies, all trying to get your attention dear. Are you disappointed that the murder wasn't for your sake?" Maggie asked him, still shaking with laughter.

"No!" he cried, "Of course not! They didn't really think that did they?!"

All eyes turned towards DS Elliot, who looked deeply uncomfortable.

"*I* didn't think that," he mumbled uneasily.

"It's alright dear," Maggie told him, "A good man in hard to come by, we all understand that."

Not everyone looked as though they understood this,

but unsurprisingly no one chose to fight Maggie on it.

"Well *we* didn't think it was about Mr Bingley," Heidi announced firmly, "we thought that it was about the thefts and blackmail in the street. We thought that Lydia had seen the thief entering the bookshop, and had followed them. We couldn't think why else she would have been in the bookshop in the middle of the night. Our whole investigation was based around that theory, but of course, we were wrong. Lydia was the one breaking in, and she was followed by someone that she had been blackmailing."

"Blackmail is horrible," Shelley commented, shaking her head.

"You can say that again," Kitty agreed with a sigh.

A few people turned to her, allowing her the chance to speak up if she chose.

"I was being blackmailed about my drinking," she told them all, head held high, "but I decided not to keep paying. I've stopped drinking and I've joined a support group. I'm not ashamed of that fact."

"Well done!" Maggie cheered, clapping her hands.

A small flurry of applause and congratulations followed, making Kitty seem to glow with happiness.

"We were being blackmailed too," Elizabeth told the group, with a quick look to Heidi for approval.

"This is where I get a bit lost," Maggie admitted.

"I asked Heidi not to say anything, but we had a

package arrive at the shop. It must have been addressed wrong, because it wasn't for us, but I didn't know how to prove that! It was full of drugs! I was terrified that we'd get in trouble, and then when Lydia was killed, I was more afraid than ever! How could I make the police understand that the drugs weren't ours and had nothing to do with a murder that happened just a few doors away?! I was sure we'd be arrested!"

"But the drugs weren't anything to do with them, they were supposed to go somewhere else in Cross Street. They were supposed to go to Mr Price. I don't know when his business changed, but it seems that over the years he sold less and less of his original collectibles and model planes, and moved further and further into drug distribution." Heidi reported.

"All those packages always coming in and going out! I just thought he was doing business by post!" Maggie exclaimed, mortified.

"Well he was, just not the business you believed. I realised that whoever was connected to the drugs had the most reason to kill the blackmailer. She could expose them! But who could be connected to drugs? And how could they know that Lydia was the blackmailer when no one else did?"

She paused, allowing the question to settle in people's minds.

"So? How did he know?!" Shelley demanded.

"That was the key. That was how I eventually realised it had to be Mr Price. I was alone in his shop a couple of days ago, and I walked into one his model planes. I called it a Cessna, but later he corrected me."

She waited for understanding but it didn't seem to come.

"How did he know I called it a Cessna?! I was alone in his shop! He had secret cameras and microphones in there to protect his drug business! He would have known exactly who the thief and blackmailer was the first time they entered his premises!"

"So he waited for an opportunity, and then followed Lydia as she entered another shop," Maggie suggested.

"Exactly. He just didn't want to attack her in his own shop, but apart from that he didn't care. He just wanted her out of the way, and for no additional attention on him or his activities."

There was silence for a moment, as no one knew what to say.

"So will Elizabeth and Jane get in trouble at all for the drugs?" Mary asked eventually.

"No, we're currently exploring the whole network of shipments, but it's clear that they weren't involved," DS Elliot assured them.

"And everyone has their things back. So it's over?"

Shelley asked hopefully.

"I suppose so," Heidi admitted, almost reluctantly.

"Not quite," Rose piped up, "I need to apologise. I know I'm not responsible for mum's actions, but someone needs to apologise to you all and she's not here to do it. I'm sorry for everything she took from you. I'm sorry she invaded your space, and stole and snooped and threatened. I'm sorry that she used your secrets against you and for all the awful things she said."

"Thank you dear," Maggie responded gently.

"Very well said," Jane agreed, smiling.

"You're nothing like your mum, you know?" Mary said quietly.

Rose looked at her, bright eyed and determined.

"I know. I don't see the world the way she did, and I don't want what she wanted. Mum hurt you worse than almost anyone. But I want to put it right."

Reaching into her tote bag, Rose pulled out a manilla envelope and handed it to a confused Mary.

"I've signed over a majority share in Luscious Whisper. It's yours. Well- ours- but mostly yours. You built that shop and you deserve it... if- if you'd be alright with sort of working together..." Rose trailed off uncertainly.

Mary stared at her for a moment, before suddenly launching herself forwards into Rose's arms, sobbing hysterically.

"I would love to! We can be partners! Real partners!"

When the emotion of the moment eventually subsided, Mary looked like a different woman, still bruised and battered, but happy and strong.

"I might not have parents, but I'm glad I have you," Rose told her sincerely.

"There's more than one kind of family dear," Maggie announced, shooting Heidi a significant look.

There absolutely is.

"Speaking of which, I'm going to need everybody's help in the near future," Maggie told them all, "I've agreed to take in a couple of exchange students for the university. It's just one term, but the young ladies are coming all the way from Australia, so I'd like us all to find some ways to make them feel welcome."

"From Australia?!" Shelley exclaimed, "that's amazing! What are they like?"

"Well one is named Gabby, and the other is Alice. That's all I know so far, but I'm certain they'll be delightful. And travelling to the other side of the world, I'm sure sure it's going to feel like they've fallen down the rabbit hole!" Maggie told them.

"Malice in wonderland!" DS Elliot added quickly through a mouthful of chocolate eclair, clearly keen to display that he had recognised the literary reference.

"What was that dear?"

"Alice! I meant Alice in wonderland," he amended.

"I certainly hope there won't be any *malice* involved!" Maggie chuckled.

Heidi felt a prickling sensation running up her spine but consciously pushed it away.

Everything was going to be fine. The murder was solved, the break-ins were over- everything was going to get back to normal.

How could it not?

More Books by Elinor Battersby

The Holly Abbot Mysteries
The First Sign Of Trouble
Just A Second, I'm Thinking
Third Place Ribbon
Go Fourth And Be Merry
A Fifth Of Scotch
Sixth House On The Left
Seventh Month

YA Thrillers
Lucky Penny
Lost Rose

BV - #0016 - 260325 - C0 - 203/127/18 - PB - 9781739571849 - Matt Lamination